Near To The  present
Knuckle Cracking Novellas
10

Portrait of an Assassin

By Richard Godwin

Copyright © 2017 by Richard Godwin

Independently Published by Near To The Knuckle

All rights reserved. This book or any portion thereof may not be reproduced or used in any manner whatsoever without the express written permission of the publisher except for the use of brief quotations in a book review.

Printed in the United Kingdom

Cover Design by Craig Douglas

Formatted and Edited by Craig Douglas

First Printing, 2017

ISBN 978-1-52121-744-3

Near To The Knuckle
Rugby
Warwickshire, CV22

www.close2thebone.co.uk

Other Great Titles From the Knuckle Cracking Novella series

1. *Bad Luck City* by Matt Phillips
2. *One Day In The Life Of Jason Dean* by Ian Ayris
3. *Marwick's Reckoning* by Gareth Spark
4. *Back To The World* by Jim Shaffer
5. *An Eye For An Eye* by Paul Heatley
6. *A Dish Served Cold* by B.R. Stateham
7. *Too Many Crooks* by Paul D. Brazill
8. *A Case Of Noir* by Paul D. Brazill
9. *Big City Blues* by Paul D. Brazill
10. *Portrait Of An Assassin* by Richard Godwin

About the Author
Richard Godwin

Richard Godwin is the critically acclaimed author of *Apostle Rising, Mr. Glamour, One Lost Summer, Noir City, Meaningful Conversations, Confessions Of A Hit Man, Paranoia And The Destiny Programme, Wrong Crowd, Savage Highway, Ersatz World, The Pure And The Hated, Disembodied, Buffalo And Sour Mash, Locked In Cages,* and *Crystal On Electric Acetate*. His stories have been published in numerous paying magazines and over 34 anthologies, among them an anthology of his stories, *Piquant: Tales Of The Mustard Man*, and The Mammoth Book Of Best British Crime and The Mammoth Book Of Best British Mystery, alongside Lee Child. He was born in London and lectured in English and American literature at the University of London. He also teaches creative writing at University and workshops. You can find out more about him at his website **www.richardgodwin.net**, where you can read a full list of his works, and where you can also read his Chin Wags At The Slaughterhouse, his highly popular and unusual interviews with other authors.

Dedication

For Page

Portrait of an Assassin

Contents

The Politician	1
The Priest	25
The Policeman	43
The Necrophiliac	53
The Arms Dealer	71
The Actor	131
The Goddess	143
The Entrepreneur	185
Klein	199

Nameless enterprises, assignations with men of secrecy, I am the Assassin, sometimes they call me a mechanic, hit man, button man, hired gun; but it is more than a gun I use, and while you may judge, there is no room for judgement in a world of diminished morality, you do what you are paid to do in this world of fiscal exchanges.

The Politician

I

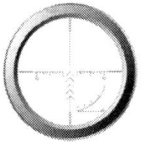

My first hit was a politician. Major league.

I was 21, and felt a hundred. I remember blowing his face off. Not the cleanest job. Nearly cost me another contract.

But I learned. Always was a fast learner. Cleaned up my act for the next one. Used the money to clear my debts, and enjoyed myself a little.

My story travels. It has mileage. It exposes a lot of lies at the top of the tree. Lies that affect you and me. Lies that the people who govern us, tell us, while they save their skins and burn our money.

You don't get that close to the real players without finding out their secrets and I got close enough to blow their breath away. I'll tell you how it all happened, and it led me right to the heart of the government.

Who am I? Ex-Military, trained marksman and explosives expert. Served with the Royal Marines as a specialist in reconnaissance and sabotage. Good at gathering information. And hiding it.

I am faceless. Assumed names are all I need. I don't know if anyone's still alive who would know my real one.

It all started with a simple job, and then it snowballed into something big, and really sinister. I was chasing a monster and it turned.

I'd travelled a lot and made some contacts. They felt they owned me and I owed them.

Recently I'd been wasting my life in casinos, on whores and I was about to find myself out on the street, again.

I'd been there before and didn't enjoy it. I'd seen enough luxury to want some, and was sick of being on the outside of it.

One bleak November morning when I wanted to rip the London skies apart, two envelopes landed on my mat.

The brown one contained a final warning on my rent arrears, the white one this:

Call me regarding previous discussions. The job is yours.

I recognised the number. I knew one day the contact would come.

***

Luca Martoni was in London on business.

I met him at his suite at the Lowndes, suitably known as London's best kept secret.

He was as I remembered him, immaculately tailored, polished and tanned, blending in with the discreet luxury of the place.

"Good to see you, Jack." He squeezed my hand and flashed his white smile at me. "Drink? Whisky, right?"

"Are we alone?"

"Of course." He'd already drawn the curtains.

He sat in a chair and swung one of his *Gucci* shoes over his other leg.

"You recall our conversation last year at my villa?"

"How could I forget?"

"You will remember, then, how we spoke of certain matters that I felt at the time you could help us with."

"I remember."

I swigged the deep golden malt.

"We need your help. I have a job, and I believe you are the man to do it."

I thought for a moment of what I was getting into. It's only the first time you do that. A bit like stepping off a precipice, checking the rope. After the first one, you concentrate on the detail: the pay-off.

I thought about the other options I still had, and the bailiffs.

"So," he said, standing up, "five now, and ten on completion."

"I don't know what the job is."

"It's a fair price, Jack. Unless, of course, you mess it up."

"In which case?"

He flashed his teeth at me. "Another whisky?"

He handed me back my glass and then opened his attaché case. "This will answer any questions you have."

He passed me a large manila envelope.

It contained photographs, maps, press cuttings, a schedule of the man's movements. And five thousand pounds in cash.

"So?"

I hesitated. I recognised the face. It had been splattered across every tabloid for weeks.

"Why?"

Leaning forward, he said, "He has defaulted on loans. Mr Stone is someone we have invested heavily in. We believed he would give good return."

"On?"

"Oh, imports, information, free publicity, that sort of thing. But he has, shall we say, been less than honourable, so there is a little score to settle."

"Information?"

"Jack, we live in a world where information is the new gold. At the same time, the old rules of the street still apply."

"You just want him taken out."

"Yes. And…" He looked at me, weighing me up.

"And?"

"If you can locate and retrieve some data, there is a bonus."

"What data?"

"A file. It's all there," he said, pointing at the envelope.

"Just run it past me anyway."

"It's clearly marked, Jack. One file. Easy to find. In it you will locate bank details including passwords. Mr Stone has been careful not to leave what we want on computer, so he's kept a manual record."

"I see."

"We feel confident that with your background you're right for this."

I knocked back the whisky.

"And the bonus?"

"Another ten. If you need anything else, let me know."

"And if I only carry out the first part of the job?"

He laid a hand on my shoulder.

"Jack, we have every confidence in you."

That day I left his hotel room with the money and the weapon, a Glock. Good gun, light trigger. It would do the job.

I made sure I was not being followed and returned to my shabby studio where I spent the evening reading through the package.

The next day I paid my arrears, much to the surprise of the letting agency.

Then I got everything I needed for the job.

I studied the target.

II

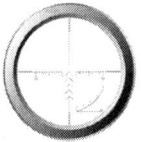

Stone had been ripping off his constituency for years, cheating on business deals, his wife and abusing his kids.

I already knew about him from the papers, which were having a field day with the fact that he'd been charged with fraud.

I carried out some preliminary stalking. His movements were exactly as the schedule gave them to be: a creature of habit, the easiest target.

He had a mistress he visited in a flat in Shepherd's Bush, probably paid for by the tax payer.

I saw him come and go with a mixture of swagger and caution. His sexual proclivities made him sloppy, an easy target to watch.

I thought about Martini's brief, knowing the information was as important as the hit.

Posing as a courier I visited his office.

A bored receptionist sat chewing gum, reading an article until I cleared my throat. She'd seen me enter, but couldn't be bothered.

As she looked up I heard the door swing behind me. She stopped chewing, looked past me and smiled.

"Good morning."

A man in a pin-striped suit brushed past me.

"Sheila, lovely day, is he up there?"

"I'll buzz him."

I clocked the floor number he pressed.

"Can I help?" she finally said, chewing loudly.

"Parcel for Mr," I paused, looking down, "Str-ack-ville," I said, sounding as stupid as I could.

"No one here by that name."

"Are you sure?"

"You've got the wrong address."

"Sorry."

The phone rang.

"Excuse me," she said, swivelling her chair, turning her back on me.

I walked to the end of the corridor and found the staircase.

The back door had a weak lock, so it would be easy to make it look like a break-in if I did the job there.

***

One evening I got a call from Martoni.

"How near are we to completion?" he asked.

"Sounds like you're talking about a house."

"What's the difference? It's all business."

"I didn't know there was a deadline."

"I leave town next week."

"I'll do my best, I'm just putting the finishing touches on."

"Stick to the remit, Jack. Do what you're paid to do."

"Some keys to Stone's office would be useful."

"I'll arrange for you to have them."

The line went dead.

I looked out of the dirty window down to the street below. Cars hissed by on the tarmac, washed clean by the rain that had been falling since the morning. Pedestrians hopped around the puddles, umbrellas up, scurrying home from work. I realised I hadn't been outside all day. The whole thing started to bother me. I felt dirty by association, and thought my only two options were completion or escape. But where would I flee to?

I decided to go out for some groceries and booze.

As I opened the door to the street two burly blokes pushed their way past me into the corridor.

"Rent collection," one of them said.

The other fished some crumpled papers out of his pocket.

"Says here you owe over a thousand pounds."

"I paid it."

"When?"

"Two days ago."

"We don't know anything about that, and besides, there's interest."

"I went into the agency and gave them the money. Call them."

The larger guy did, hanging up after a few seconds.

"Office's shut."

"We need the money," the other one said.

"Or what?"

"We take what you've got."

"Well, that's not much."

"If you don't mind, we'll go and have a look."

They were starting up the stairs, when I thought of the Glock in my flat.

"Look, how much interest are you saying I owe?"

"Two hundred."

"What?"

"It's all in the paperwork," the big guy said, scratching his arse.

"I can give it to you, and then tomorrow you can ring the agents and clear all this up."

He shook his head.

"Nothing to do with us. We need it all now. You'll 'ave to get a refund off the agent."

"That's crap, I've paid them."

"How do we know that?" They were almost upstairs now. "Are you going to let us in?"

"OK, come with me. I'll get you the money now."

"Where?"

"The cashpoint."

"You've got it all?"

"Yes."

"You'll 'ave to sign this," he said, handing me the paper, "and you better not be messing us around."

I doodled all over it and passed it back to him.

"Is that really the best they can do? Send two heavies round when I've paid my rent."

"They said you could be trouble. And how do we know you've paid?"

"The bank's round the corner."

"How far?"

"Five minutes."

"We'll drive."

"You won't be able to park. It's a red route and it's quicker on foot."

They'd done me a favour. I wasn't going to live like this anymore.

Once I'd got them out on the street, it was easy. I took them into a back alley saying it was a short cut and swinging round, floored the big one first. He was overweight and quickly dropped to his knees clutching his groin while I took care of his colleague.

He was slow and missed me. It was an easy duck.

As I came up I hit him with a right hook that took him straight out.

By now the other guy was coming up for air, so I kicked him hard until he stopped moving.

I went back, stuck everything I had in a couple of bags and left the flat. The bus was pulling away when I saw the two guys lumbering back down the road.

I booked into a hotel two streets away from Stone's offices and started my new life that night. I never saw the bailiffs again.

I gave Martoni my new address, and the keys dutifully arrived. Alone and totally outside the lives of everyone I'd ever known, I watched my prey.

I sat in cafes planning the hit, while couples and workers came and went in another world.

I was looking at life through a telescopic lens, squaring the heart of the cross with the target.

I was planning the final stages. Making sure it would be just me and him when I did it. I knew his life. I could almost predict what he would do next. At night I searched his office.

I went through every drawer, and realised the file I needed was not kept there.

Blowing him away gave me access to what Martoni wanted, but Stone was holding the information. He was a hands-on guy: he'd already dipped his fingers in the public till, and I figured he'd keep what he valued close to him.

I'd seen him coming and going and he always carried the same attaché case with him. My guess was he kept his most confidential papers in there.

I was motivating myself to do it. To take him out.

Effective killing is about a trained mind. Your hand might hold the gun, but the mind pulls the trigger. I was moving into a zone I'd been conditioned in, closing in like a shadow silently crossing Stone's path. I was zeroing in on him. Taking aim.

Still a stranger he was becoming familiar, becoming a reality. A reality my remit was to end.

***

One afternoon, I went into the square at the back of Stone's offices. I watched his movements from there.

A boy ran across the grass.

He was crying and his face was stained with tears.

I guessed he was about five.

A man on the other side of the square was calling him.

"Adam. Come here!"

The boy dutifully turned and ran towards him. Stone.

He stood by the gates, hands in overcoat pockets, waiting for his son.

"Shut up, you little crybaby. Look at you! How could you be my son? God knows who that whore of a mother of yours was screwing when you were born."

"Daddy you said I could have a balloon on my birthday."

He grabbed the boy by the arm and started walking him towards his car. I could see his face clearly through the railings as they passed. It was knotted with fury and disdain.

"Birthday!? Grow up! Now get in the car."

With that he threw him into the back and drove off.

I looked at my watch: 6 o'clock. He saw his mistress at half-past.

I got there before him and watched him walk in with his swagger and the usual bunch of roses. He was sticking to the routine I knew now. It was strange, sharing his movements, as if I was willing him towards his end.

He left two hours later smoking his cigar and headed into town to eat.

Through the restaurant window I saw a man dripping with charm and joke his way through several bottles of vintage champagne. With his large hands he gestured and dominated the conversation.

On one side of the glass he looked content and full.

On the other side I had all I needed.

III

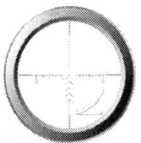

I planned to do it the next night.

His wife would be out and he would get home after screwing his mistress. That gave me a window of two hours in which to end his life and make it look like a break-in.

I decided this was the best disguise for the hit, since the offices would draw too much attention to his death.

That was the plan, anyway.

I checked out of my hotel and into another way across town. I collected what I needed and went over the plan again. The next day I hot-wired and hid a car. Then I waited.

The morning dragged poisonously into the afternoon and finally I watched darkness settle. When the birds stopped singing I felt a strange sort of calm, almost serenity. As if I only had one option now, and that gave my fractured life some sort of cohesion. Like when a plane takes off, there's no going back to check if you've left the gas on.

I parked around the block, made my way into his garden and waited.

The kitchen window was open and provided easy access.

He was late.

I had reckoned nine, but it was ten before I heard the car pull up.

I crouched beneath a tree waiting for a sighting, and then saw his wife walk into the kitchen.

She threw her coat onto the floor and fixed herself a drink.

My head span.

Then another car crunched the gravel at the front.

The sound of heavy footsteps.

I saw Stone enter the kitchen. He put his attaché case on the table.

They started arguing, and I could hear every word.

"It's not what you think."

"You fucker!"

"It's just sex!"

"I've heard that before."

"I'll ditch her. You're the woman I love."

"You bastard."

"Oh come on, Sam."

"Don't Sam me."

"I'll ring her now and tell her it's off."

"I mean for Christ's sake, you can't even make it to your son's birthday. You don't care about anyone, do you?"

"I know, I know, I'll make it up to him, I had a meeting. What can I do?"

"Make an effort, you shit." She poured herself another drink. "I mean it's not enough that you go and rip off the taxpayer and have us hassled by paparazzi, you have to go and fuck every two-bit tart in sight. What is it? Can't you think with your brain, instead of your prick?"

She was getting wilder with the drink, and Stone started to pace the kitchen.

"I work every hour under the sun to provide you with the lifestyle you need, and all you have to do is entertain once in a while."

"You said you'd never do that to me again."

"I'm sorry."

"You fucker."

She threw her drink in his face and poured another one.

Stone walked over to the sink, feet from where I watched.

I could see his jowly face and he was angry. The veins on his temple were standing out, and his hands shook as he wiped the vodka away.

"Don't do that again," he said, turning his back to the window.

"Or what?"

"I'm warning you."

"What are you going to do? Beat me up?"

"Let's just forget the whole thing."

"No! How would you like it if I was unfaithful?"

"You're not though."

"Aren't I?"

"You're not the type."

"Oh really?"

"What is that supposed to mean?"

"Let me inform you, Mr fucking Stone, because that's what you are, a fucking stone, a heartless piece of shit, that I have been having an affair of my own."

"You're drunk."

"I have been fucking, or been fucked by a beautiful young man, and guess what, he makes me come. I don't have to fake orgasm with him."

"I've had enough of this."

He was moving toward the kitchen door.

"He can satisfy a woman. He doesn't have to pay her, like you do your tart."

"I said enough!"

He spun round and hit her.

It was a hard backhand slap that knocked her against the counter.

She steadied herself and poured another drink.

"I could get you arrested," she said, suddenly calm now.

"Look, I could be going down, you fucking little bitch."

She walked right up to him.

"You don't like it, do you? Another man with your wife, his prick inside me, and I loved it, I ate him up."

They were standing inches from each other.

"You've had enough to drink," he said, grabbing her glass.

"No I haven't."

She wrestled with him and finally it fell, shattering on the flagstone floor.

She walked over to the cabinet and got another one.

"You know, it's interesting, the more vodka I drink, the more truthful I become."

"You have a problem."

"Yes, you. And another thing, I'm leaving you."

"Oh no, you're not."

"You can get some other fucker to do your bloody dinner parties."

"I've given you everything you wanted."

"You never gave me children."

A moment's silence stretched like a tightrope.

"What?"

"They're not yours. You've been bringing up another man's kids, and, you know what, you deserve it, you fucking loser."

Stone walked over to the kitchen table. He picked up his gloves and put them on.

"Running away?"

"Oh no," he said.

He made a fist, turned round slowly, and hit her.

It was a hard blow and she knocked her head against the wall with a loud crack.

He hit her again, and again. He hit her in the face, the wall breaking the momentum of her head.

Her body slumped, leaving a thick smear of blood on the magnolia wallpaper.

He leaned over to check her pulse, then left the room.

I waited for what seemed like an eternity for him to return, wishing I'd picked his office.

He'd changed his clothes and was carrying a holdall.

He came out into the garden and, locking the back door from the outside, kicked it in. Then he started to mess up the house.

I waited until he was in the living room when I seized my moment.

Two people could use the cover of a break-in.

Treading carefully to avoid the pool of blood, I sidestepped his wife's body.

He was emptying drawers onto the floor. I was almost upon him when he caught my reflection in the mirror.

"What the-?" he said, and swung at me.

I ducked and coming up, I pressed the muffler against his face.

I had never intended to get so close, but this was spinning out of control. I just had to end it.

"Who are you? What do you want?"

I squeezed the Glock and blew his face away. Literally.

His cheek and nose shot across the room, adding to the décor, sticking like lumps of meat to the flock wallpaper. He fell heavily onto the thick carpet with a peephole to his brains in his face. There were fragments of his skin and vein everywhere.

After I cleaned myself up, I went into the kitchen. His case was still on the table.

It lay open, and all I needed to do was reach inside and pull the file out.

I didn't have to make anymore mess, he'd done that for me.

IV

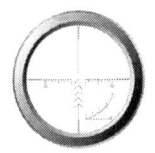

When I handed Martoni the file, the white smile broke across his face like a scar. "I always said we have every confidence in you, Jack."

I sat in the same chair as on the first meeting.

"This is for you," he said, passing me an envelope.

I didn't even bother checking its contents.

After a whisky I left.

"We will be in touch, and, well done," he said.

In the elevator down I glanced inside: 25k in readies.

***

I wanted the money and out. I thought I would travel and get my head together, maybe start up my own business. Put a deposit down on a place and pick up my life again.

There's a difference between an order and a brief. The difference of choice, or the choices people think they're making. Sometimes that might just mean letting other people call the shots. Deferring to authority. Copping out.

The horizon had shifted and the sky looked bloodshot. All it took was the blink of an eye in which I blew Stone's breath away.

I wanted to clear the experience out of my throat.

But when I looked in the mirror there was someone else staring back at me. Someone through life took on the grainy separate quality of a slow-motion film; as though moving on ice.

If I thought my first job was complicated I was in for a ride on a well-greased helter skelter. My hands were about to get a whole lot dirtier.

***

A few nights later the phone went. It was Martoni.

"Jack. A few questions."

"Yes?"

"Why the mess?"

"Unavoidable."

"His face was all over the gun."

"It got complicated."

"Please. Explain."

"The office was never going to be the place, it had to be at his house."

"And his wife dies too?"

"I had it planned. She turns up, wise to his affair and they start a domestic."

"Did you kill her?"

"Stone did."

"OK."

"I made it look like a break-in. Unfortunately, he was quicker than I expected and I had to pop him from close range."

There was a long pause. I could hear him breathing.

"It's your first hit. We'll be in touch."

The Priest

V

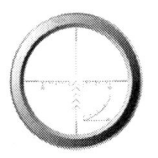

Travelling around Europe, when I left the Royal Marines had brought me many experiences.

Having no family contacts, I was unconstrained by the usual ties.

I drifted around the Greek islands, picking up casual bar work as I went, and eventually decided to explore Italy.

It seemed logical to drift south, and one day I landed in Sicily.

Straying away from the big towns like Palermo and craving solitude I ventured into the interior of the island. I'd resolved to get my head together and then head back to London in pursuit of employment.

I rented a room over a crumbling hotel with only a handful of rooms in a tiny place called Pietraperzia. What bustle of activity that occurred beneath the blistering sun soon settled into a habitual quiet, giving me time to think. By day the local youths revved their motorbikes outside my window, while night time brought the parade of locals, and then a deathly silence.

I sat and drank too much, or explored the neighbouring countryside.

One evening, as I went out to eat, a fight broke out.

I was passing a back alley which overflowed with

rubbish and heard a man crying out.

Two guys were knocking the shit out of him.

I walked into the alley and as I got close one of them swiped at me.

I dodged, spotting the duster, and managed to drop him.

The other one pulled out a gun.

He came right up to me and held it inches away.

I started to back off and caught him in the groin with a kick. He crumpled, winded, while I beat him unconscious, flinging his piece into the garbage.

I quickly got the injured man out of there and understood enough Italian to make out he had a car nearby. Then I drove him into the countryside, following his directions which consisted of pointing and banging the dashboard.

It was a new Mercedes, which was unusual for that area, as it was fairly poor.

Finally, we pulled up outside a large, gated villa.

He buzzed me in and that is how I made my introduction to Luca Martoni.

After tending to his younger brother and offering me a glass of wine, he shook my hand and thanked me.

"You have saved his life, Jack, and I will remember you for it. You were good. Army?"

"No, not Army, Royal Marines."

"Oh. Good."

"How do I get back to my hotel from here?"

He shook his head.

"You do not understand."

"Understand what?"

"The men you fought earlier will be looking for you. You stay here now, you are our guest. In the morning I will send some people to fetch your things."

"It's OK, I can handle myself."

"Look, Jack, they will have to kill you. You are in a foreign land without anyone to help you, apart from my family. Don't be foolish."

"What have I got involved with?"

"I will explain. But another time. Now it is late, let me show you to your room."

He led me up a flight of stairs to a large well appointed bedroom with an ensuite. The trappings of wealth were everywhere. It certainly beat any other accommodation round there.

For the rest of my time in Sicily, I stayed at his villa in Camitrice, a tiny settlement of houses between two towns. It is not even on many maps.

I learned about Martoni and the business he conducted, and he made it clear that as much as he was grateful to me for saving his brother's life, I was being inducted.

He wanted to know about my military training. He introduced me to some of his people, killers and hustlers, businessmen and heavies.

I spent lazy days around his pool, taking in the timeless landscape, lost among the olive groves. And then one day I decided to leave.

VI

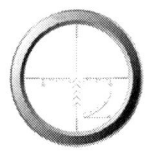

Once you start, you get sucked into another life.

Killing is addictive, the habits around assassination are themselves habit forming.

After Stone I travelled around for a while, staying in one hotel after another.

Enjoying the money, I deluded myself that was it and I would seek a new direction. The truth is, I'd already found it.

It wasn't long before Martoni made contact again.

He was back in London and I met him the next day.

He got right down to business.

"This time, the profile is different, Jack."

I went through the file and was baffled. Clipping after clipping of church affairs, mostly in Italian; picture after picture of a priest at different stages in his life. A young man being promoted within the ranks of the Catholic church. Growing old. Getting status.

Martoni sat waiting.

"I can see you are perplexed."

"What reason is there for killing this man?"

"The church is highly organised, and useful at times. People follow its message, especially in poor, uneducated communities, their belief is all they have to sustain them."

"Forgive me, but where is this leading?"

"Power, Jack. Power."

"A highly regarded man of the cloth, who you want dead."

"Not me personally, but he deserves it."

"That's the bit I'm missing. I get the bit about how the church works. Business as usual."

"Yes, business. Well, Jack, there is another business, Father Anthony has been involved in, which has been covered up by the church. He has been moved sideways, and protected by those very high up. Very high up."

"What are we talking about?"

"Child abuse. The man is a paedophile." He got up and poured me a drink. "The reason all the file contains is a background and various pictures you may find useful in order to identify him is because it has been so effectively covered up, the press haven't got wind of it. He has been abusing children since he was a young priest. He has ruined lives and used his position of trust to indulge his perversion. Your remit is to kill a paedophile."

"He's been doing this for years, you say."

"Yes."

"Your - client."

"My client's children were both abused by him. The legacy of his actions, the threats he placed them under, the psychological as well as physical damage he has caused them is never going to go away. The boy took his own life last month, the girl is in a mental institution, probably for life. He had raped her repeatedly, often using a crucifix, and now, you know what his favourite sermon is?" I shrugged. "The value of forgiveness."

"Some things are unforgivable."

"I agree entirely."

"And the two kids you mention are the tip of the iceberg."

"Who knows how many he has abused? Hundreds."

"The biggest preachers of forgiveness are often those who want to cut themselves the most slack."

"The job will take place in Rome."

"Before the bastard becomes Pope."

There was the smile again, and then I was gone.

This time there would be no gun.

I had something else in store for Father Anthony. And when I had finished he would no longer need to struggle with temptation.

VII

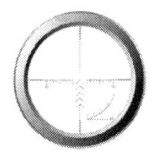

Rome was a bustle of activity and noise.

I checked into the Intercontinental on the outskirts, equidistant between the airport and Father Anthony's house.

He lived in a wealthy neighbourhood not far from his church, a huge Renaissance indulgence, where he lorded it over the other priests.

Paying a visit there, I saw him and hated him on sight.

As I sat taking it in, deciding where to carry out the hit, he passed me.

He swished his robes and started to lecture another priest in Italian.

He was a fat, bloated man with a high-pitched voice. An epicene bully who smelt of rose water and incense. Every so often as he talked, he would fiddle with his crucifix, running his pale fingers down the shaft. He disappeared shortly after shouting his orders, but I'd seen all I needed. There was something unwholesome about him, a stench I couldn't drive away for several hours.

I carried out what surveillance I needed, checking out his house, a wealthy villa more suited to a businessman. I wanted to kill him and leave before he had a chance to abuse more children. And all the time I kept seeing him fiddle with his cross.

I didn't want to get too close, since Martoni had said no gun.

Watching him leave one morning I saw him get into a BMW. It would provide me with the ideal hit for him.

I'd been taught a few tricks from friends in the Royal Engineers about explosives. I had a knack for demolitions and this wouldn't be any different. The priest lived far enough away from the life of the city for it not to be a risk to anyone else.

I made a few calls. Martoni had given me some contacts in the city who he said would help me out.

***

Marco Latressa was a small man with a heavily scarred face, and I met him at the *Piazza San Pietro*.

"Mr Jack," he said, offering me a strong handshake.

"Lucas filled you in?"

"Everything, I know what you need. From your telephone conversation, I ascertain much, is that correct English?"

"Yes."

"Good, I always say, language is the first step towards a better world."

"And the second?"

He laughed.

"You are here, aren't you? The world is full of hyenas and wolves."

"So, do you have access to the materials?"

"Come."

He drove me to a quiet road some kilometres away and parked outside a disused shop.

In a back room all the materials I needed were laid out on a table, pipe, watch, wires, semtex.

I needed to get Father Anthony in his car at the right time.

I watched him and worked out his movements.

He always gave a heavy sermon on a Sunday. Preached about Satan's grip on the modern world and the breakdown in family values. He would later return to his house and visit families, locally. And usually on foot. He rarely used his car, but would go shopping for groceries once a week and pay a visit to a family on the outskirts of the city every Tuesday afternoon.

I figured he was abusing or grooming the kids. He took them sweets and spent time alone with them. He would return in a good mood and take a long bath before going to church. The timing on this hit was critical.

One morning, watching his house from my car, I saw him coming out to talk to his housekeeper. She was late and he was admonishing her for her timekeeping. His voice was loud and carried in the still air. The woman, in her sixties, curtsied to him, and he dismissed her with a wave.

Some English tourists, obviously lost, passed by with maps as he was about to go back inside.

"Scusi, do you speak English?" one of them asked.

He stopped and turned to look at them. A man with a rucksack with two women, one wearing a vest, the other shorts and a T-shirt.

"Ye-es, I speak da English," he said, modulating his tone.

Shallow charm oozed from him like grease.

They were trying to find a church. The man fumbled with a map, while Father Anthony ignored him.

"Ye-es, it is not far," he said, looking at the

women. "But you cannot go there like this."

"Like what?" the woman in the vest said.

"That," he said, prodding her in the chest.

"Hey, wait a minute, what do you think you're doing?"

"Your breasts are on display, and you want to go into a church. Are you a prostitute?"

"You're out of order. If I want to dress…"

"No! You are in Italy, you silly girl. Your nipples are exposed, do you have no shame?"

The man was unsure what to do, and the other woman got involved now.

"Hold on, you can't speak to her like that."

"Another prostitute? All you English women are the same, sleep with anyone, get drunk. Mary Magdalene-".

"I'm not interested in Mary Magdalene," she said. "We asked for directions, we're in your country, I wish we hadn't."

"Yes, you are in my country, and you behave like filthy whores. You expose your flesh, your bodies you have no respect for, and you as a man, are you not ashamed to be seen with these - aah!"

"You have no right to speak to them like that," the guy said. "In England we've moved into the twenty-first century you know."

The woman in the vest was angry.

"You might think you're appointed by God, but I don't, we just wanted to look at the architecture."

"You asked my advice."

"No. We asked directions. You stand there and moralise me about how I dress. It's my body, I choose who I let see it, who I let touch it, you creep!"

"Everyone see it!" he said.

And with that he reached out and pulled her vest

down momentarily so that her breasts were exposed before the material snapped back.

The group was speechless and just stood there while he turned and entered his villa, locking the gate after him.

The woman in the vest was seething.

"I'm going to report him."

"Dirty old man, that's sexual assault," her friend said.

The man stood there staring at the villa.

After a while, they drifted away looking dazed.

I would do it next Tuesday, before he paid another visit to those kids.

***

I spent Monday organising my departure. I had a ticket for the following afternoon.

In the evening I put together the bomb over at the disused shop.

I had a light meal and a walk.

At two o'clock in the morning I left. There was no night porter and no one to see me leave.

I hot-wired a car and drove round to Father Anthony's house. It was dark. I sat a hundred metres away, checking for late revellers, frequency of traffic. It was as quiet as I'd figured it would be.

Parking around the back in a small side road, I donned my balaclava. Then I walked to his car which was parked outside his villa.

Checking for signs of life and seeing none, I started work.

I got underneath and managed to attach the bomb with tape in just under two minutes. Then I activated it.

The next time the ignition was turned it would blow. There were no other cars parked nearby.

When I resurfaced the street was as quiet as a grave. I headed back to my car and left, dumping it in a yard some distance from the hotel.

***

The next day at ten to one I parked at the edge of his street. I could see his car and was far enough away not to be seen from any of the houses.

I waited.

At ten past, he came out. He was carrying some bags of sweets. As he walked, he fiddled with his crucifix. He stopped, fumbling in his pockets.

Then, sweetly, he got in.

There was a delay.

What he was doing?

A car drove down the street and I hoped he would stall.

It passed him, turning left at the end. I sat there willing him to start the engine, wondering what he was doing.

A woman walked past and waved at him. I saw his arm wave back out of the window. She disappeared into one of the houses, and still I waited.

Had the engine failed?

Then I heard it.

I felt it first, a heavy shove, then the noise followed.

In slow motion, bits of his car flew down the road. A door slammed down on the other side, flames and fragments of metal showering the street. A wheel bounced down the road towards me. Windows from nearby houses began to break.

I reversed out of there just as a few startled women emerged from their houses, pressing their hands to their faces, clutching their skirts.

I returned to my hotel, got my bags and paid.

At the airport I found a bar and waited to board.

The Policeman

VIII

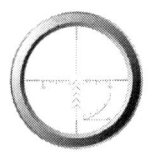

I picked up my pay-cheques, and each time the amount went up.

I was getting a reputation. My speed and efficiency were often referred to by Martoni, who began to put me onto other contacts. Work streamed in and like any business, once the momentum started, it kept going so long as I was as good as my last job.

Martoni complimented me on the hits I'd carried out.

"You are clean and follow the remit."

"Everyone loves a clean hit," I said, looking over my shoulder for the person I used to be.

I bought a place which I rarely used since I was travelling so much. The lifestyle changes you. You need to be displaced for it to work.

I was walking toward something so tangled and twisted I was going to need something a lot sharper than wire cutters to get out.

I carried out the hits and collected the money. I became known. Other predators began to size me up. They watched from their world, hemmed in with lies that twisted like barbed wire. They were invisible. They inhabited a criminal world outside the reaches of the legal system.

I wondered when Martoni would want me to deal with a problem in his own back yard and I didn't have long to wait.

A police chief in Sicily wasn't playing ball with the Mafia.

***

I headed back to the interior, and booked into a smart hotel near the town where this guy Trappatoni was causing so much trouble.

Dante Rossi, a key family figure, briefed me and provided my point of contact while there.

A muscular heavy man who liked his pasta, he squeezed my hand as hard as he could when he met me, and when I squeezed back he grinned with the glow of satisfied machismo.

"Jack, it is an honour to meet you," he said, conducting me inside his well-equipped villa.

We sat down with a couple of drinks and went through the hit.

"Luca informs me you believe shooting is not the way here."

"That's right," I said, sipping the cold glass of *Asti*.

It was summer and temperatures had already reached the high thirties.

He leaned forward.

"We need to send out a message. This is all about territory."

"I understand, and I have a way of getting that message through, loud and clear. Sometimes you need to startle people out of their complacency."

"I li-ike this, yes."

"So, you leave the hit to me, and fill me in with what I need to know."

"He live two kilometre from the police offices."

"Family?"

"Wife, two daughters."

"I need access to him when he will be alone, and I need maps."

"It's all here, Jack. So far as access is concerned, he work late at the police, ow you say?"

"Station."

"Station, yes. He work late Friday. With family, is hard, because wife always there and daughters after school much of the time."

"So it looks like he'll die at work."

"Si."

"What's the security like?"

"We ave keys. We ave da inside man."

"Good."

"We want to put a comrade in his position."

"Can I see the maps?"

There were only two ways into the station. The front was out of the question. The back door led into the passage by Trappatoni's office.

"He always works late on a Friday?"

"Almost always."

"Weapons?"

"Gun."

This wasn't going to be straightforward.

***

Surveillance showed me that the first part of the job had been well taken care of. Rossi was right. He kept pretty much to the habits I'd been given.

My first sighting of him showed me that the guy was tougher than the previous targets. About six one, boxer's nose, he'd lifted weights, and looked like he knew how to fight.

If I was going to get close, I'd need to hit him hard the first time. I decided on a traditional Mafia style weapon, which would not only disable him fast enough, but also send out a clear message, since that was what this was all about.

He was not popular with his other officers, that was clearly visible.

He lorded it over them and barked orders. They treated him with the sort of respect born of equal dislike and most of the time looked like they just wanted to get home.

By chance, I encountered him in the piazza of a local town.

By day deserted, at night wooden chairs were arranged in a circle for all the old men and local figures to sit and drink. Men only. It was like stepping back a hundred years.

I was walking through the piazza as the chairs were being set out, and he was talking to an old man.

Noticing me, he spoke to me in Italian.

"Sorry," I said.

I didn't want to get into conversation with him and started to move off, when he switched to English.

"Here as tourist?" he said.

"Yes."

"You like Sicily?"

"Very nice."

"You not football hooligan?"

"No."

"You no like football?"

"It's all right."

"All right?" he said, and broke into a laugh.

The old man obviously didn't understand a word of this and was looking a little perturbed.

Trappatoni explained to him in Italian that I was from England, then added, "These English scum come here and fuck our women, I'd like to chop their cocks off. They can't play football either, and if they do, they fly badly and end up like bolognese."

They stood there laughing.

"My friend here says he loves your country," he said.

And with that I was dismissed. He turned his back and walked off with the old man.

I'd decided before I landed not to let on that I spoke Italian and understood Sicilian.

***

Late one evening, after everyone had left, I went into the station.

I wanted to rehearse the hit, make sure there were no unseen angles.

The idea of doing a police officer in his own station was still a little uncomfortable to me.

No one was around and the area was deserted.

I disabled the security cameras and went in by the back. Then I looked around his office. My torch showed me that he was a messy worker. Files were strewn everywhere, together with unwashed cups of coffee and food wrappers.

A picture of his wife lay buried under some papers and on the wall was a framed photograph of him with some Sicilian politician. Their fixed smiles had backhanders etched into them.

I checked the drawers. He had a gun in there and

some *grappa*.

The other offices were neat and orderly testimony to the dedication and professionalism of his underdogs.

Files were stored systematically, papers allotted their place in various trays, and nothing seemed out of place.

Trappatoni's desk faced the door to his office, so approaching him from the rear was going to be hard. I needed a distraction.

It was midsummer.

The countryside was browning to a hardness under the sun.

The heat created a stillness that caught your throat as you stepped out of air conditioned cars or buildings.

There is a shadow of menace and violence steeped in the landscape in these parts of Sicily, as if years of bloodshed have had their impact on the geology.

While I was there, something happened that left me in no doubt what kind of man Trappatoni was.

A local shopkeeper, used to giving protection money to the mob, refused to inform on one of them. Trappatoni was flexing his muscles, involved in political power plays which he hoped would result in a destabilisation of Mafia power in the region. Meanwhile, he had his own protection racket going.

Locals who refused to recognise the shift in power he was attempting and stuck to the devil they knew were refused police help. Crimes were left for days without police investigation and if someone was being particularly uncooperative or represented a serious obstacle in his agenda, Trappatoni would have them burgled.

Nothing much was ever taken, but just enough damage was caused to send out a warning shot.

I'd seen the set up at his house and dismissed it as

being unsuitable for the hit. Too many people around.

His wife, who was younger than him, had the hang-dog look of a woman worn down by years of hard work and orders. Trappatoni would sit around the villa barking orders at her and at night demand sex.

I waited for the Friday night when I would do it and kept a low profile.

***

His officers left at around six.

By seven on Friday he was alone, going through papers and making his personal calls.

I turned up at half-past.

There was a back alley which served as the perfect escape route, leading out onto a deserted road where I parked the motorbike Rossi gave me.

I could see Trappatoni through the window.

He was pacing his office on the phone, shouting and waving his hand about.

Slowly, I turned the key in the back door, pausing at each notch in the mechanism.

Once inside, I waited in the corridor. He'd come out and walked into the main part of the station. A few minutes later I saw him return with a coffee. Then I heard his voice.

Once it fell quiet again, I waited and inched my way round to where I could see him.

His feet stuck out from the bottom of the desk, and I knew any attempt to get to him while he sat there would fail. For what I had planned I needed his back to me.

Finally, he stood up. I heard a chair being pushed aside. Then there was the noise of a drawer opening and I guessed that he was going through the filing cabinet.

I was right.

I entered his office unseen.

He was leaning over the second drawer, swearing in Sicilian.

I moved quickly to within inches of him as he straightened up.

For one second he stared at the reflection of a stranger in the room, and as he opened his mouth I swung the cheese wire round his thick neck.

He was a heavy man and pushed back against me as the metal dug into his flesh, quickly tearing its way through skin and vein.

He kicked up against the filing cabinet trying to throw me off, but I held him firm.

He tried to hit me, to kick me, but by then I'd severed his carotid artery.

It was like slicing meat. When I stopped, he slumped to the floor, his neck open like a piece of steak.

His blood was gathering in a thick tide, so I messed up the office a little and cleaned myself up in the police toilets.

I grabbed my hold-all from outside and changed my clothes, then I broke the door in.

I drove to Rossi's, where I burned the clothes I killed him in.

The next morning, by the time the news of another Mafia hit on a police officer reached the papers, I was on the plane back.

The Necrophiliac

IX

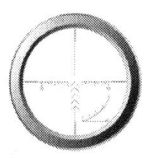

I flogged my flat making a huge profit and bought another one, which again I hardly ever used. I was more used to hotel rooms.

Martoni always called on my mobile. I would buy one every few weeks and then chuck it.

Business was good. I honed my skills. Meanwhile the line of barbed wire stretched its way round my life like a shadow.

***

My clients came from various walks of life, not all criminal. Usually they had some sob story, a jealous wife, a husband who'd found out his wife was screwing someone else. The whole tangle of other people's love lives, insurance policies, twisted motives and endless self-justification was an area I put up a no entry sign to from the word go.

I wanted professional jobs where emotions were not running high and I wouldn't be landed with some snivelling partner piqued by a late attack of conscience after their spouse had snuffed it. Court was one place I intended to stay well away from. I turned a lot of these jobs down and soon stopped getting inquiries about them.

One day I was called by a man who referred to himself as Mr Jones.

It wasn't unusual to get people wary of giving their real names and I usually found out who they were pretty quickly too.

"I've been given your number in connection with a certain business."

The voice on the other end of the line was hesitant, nervous. He was out of his depth.

"Yes."

"I believe you can take care of it for me."

"It depends what it is," I said.

I vetted everything that didn't come direct from Martoni.

I suggested we meet.

The next day by the Italian pond in Hyde Park, I watched as an anxious middle-aged man in a grey raincoat paced at the other end.

I slowly approached and suggested we walk away from the crowds.

"Good idea," he said, stuffing his unread paper in his coat pocket.

Giving him a cursory glance over, I almost chuckled.

The coat was so new it still had a label sticking out of the upturned collar. He looked like something out of an old spy movie.

We walked and I asked him what the job was.

"Have you heard of Pike and sons?"

I shook my head.

"Should I have?"

"No reason," he said. "They are well known in their line of business, which sort of overlaps with yours, but…"

"Which is?"

"What?"

"What is their line of business?"
"Funeral directors."
"Hardly the same."
"Yes. Of course. Well, they are a well known branch of funeral directors. Very well to do, good reputation. My family have used them for years. My grandmother was buried through them, my aunts, and more recently, my parents, and finally my wife."

I was beginning to mark his card as a nutter.

"What's the pitch?" I said.
"The? Ah. Yes, I see. They are as I said very reputable, and may I add, very wealthy."
"I guess it's a good business to be into."
"Yes. Well, that brings me to it, you see. They are not, or not deserving of it."
"Of what?"
"Their reputation."
"Look, Mr-?"
"Jones."
"Yeah. What is it they've done? Dropped a coffin? Lost someone's ashes?"
"Oh, far worse", he said looking at me, "far, far worse, if it was only that, I wouldn't be here now. No, I don't know how to bring myself to speak of what they have done. I am not someone who has taken this step lightly, and I had great difficulty finding someone like you. But I felt that all things considered, yes, and I have considered all angles of this shocking case, that this was the only way to get justice for my dear dead wife. God knows who else, God knows who else they've done this to, or worse."

The guy was exasperating me. He'd run out of steam and stopped to catch his breath.

"What have they done?" I said.
He paused.

"They have been selling organs from the corpses and burying sand. They have been leasing corpses to necrophiliacs."

I hadn't seen that one coming.

"No shit?"

"They have probably been doing it for years, which explains the Porsches Mr Pike and his son drive around in, the villas abroad. Oh I know a good deal about them, I have done my research, I can assure you."

"That's good."

"The black market in stolen organs is enormous, did you know? Here", he said, passing me a newspaper clipping which read:

Lack of organ donors is creating an underworld of traders.

I glanced at it and handed it back to him.

"Do you have proof?"

"Yes."

"What?"

"My wife had to be moved. The cemetery was being bulldozed. Pike was away on holiday. When the company I hired lifted her out, they dropped the coffin, a clumsy occurrence admittedly, but one for which I am grateful to them, because without it, I would never have suspected Pike. Sand fell out, and they called me."

"Were the police contacted?"

"No. I knew it would lead to a dead end. I know I am an eccentric man, but I am a realist," he said. "Kitty was everything to me, and I swore revenge from that moment on. As I stood there, in the pouring rain, staring down at the sand washing away my faith and my hope, something turned in me, I swore I would ensure that the men responsible for this atrocity were punished. But first I carried out my research."

"This wasn't a one-off? Some weird mistake?"

He shook his head.

"I am not a rash man, an accountant by profession, an accountant by nature, I love nothing better than to balance the books."

"What other evidence do you have?"

"My wife's body was offered to a necrophiliac ring. For two weeks after I buried her, she was subjected to every form of physical abuse imaginable. Then her organs were removed before the body itself, before what remained of it was cremated."

"I need more than your word."

"I know, and I can show you the evidence I have. And it's not just my dear Kitty I suspect they did it to."

"I'm sure they didn't just pick her."

"I'm an accountant and I have seen their books, I have seen their returns, the flow of finance doesn't make any sense."

"I need more evidence."

"And I will give it to you."

We arranged to meet that evening. He would return in his car and show me what he had.

"I need your help," he said. "What Pike and sons have done to my family doesn't bear speaking about."

Then I watched him walk off in the rain.

***

That evening a car pulled up at the corner of the road I'd told him to meet me on. I was standing a few feet off, and watched him slow down.

I looked at my watch. He was punctual.

I got in and directed him to a deserted car park where he stopped the car and pulled a stack of papers out of a briefcase.

There were accounts, pictures, newspaper clippings, and business receipts.

It became clear pretty quickly that he was a thorough man, who had gone to painstaking lengths to capture enough information about Pike and sons to set them up for a good law suit. I wondered why he didn't do that, and then watched him crying over the pictures of his dead wife, or what had been left of her when they sold off the final pieces.

A photograph of a stiff and formal young woman adorned the front of the file. Kitty was a throwback to the Victorian era, when wives performed their duties and husbands looked after them.

I stared briefly at the picture of another world: two people I had no point of reference to, but who had obviously loved each other very much. I wondered what that felt like.

"Bastard, bastards." He was punching the upholstery with small white hands that had never hit anything bigger than a calculator. "I want him dead. Dead! Do you understand?"

I said nothing and continued leafing through the files.

They'd certainly chopped up someone's body. Was it Kitty's?

Had Mr Jones ever been married, and what was his real name?

The incisions looked like surgical cuts into flesh entrances in order to remove organs, sure enough, and the pictures certainly showed the crime he was claiming, but against who?

I needed to check him out.

The necrophiliac plot would be hard to substantiate, but organ theft could warrant the job.

Finally, in exasperation, he cried, "What else do you need?"

"Leave it with me a few days, Mr Jones, and I'll get back to you."

"All right."

"And I need an address."

He scribbled something on a piece of paper. I would find out his real name.

"And this will cost."

"My Kitty is worth any price. How much?"

"Sixty."

"Agreed."

"I'll call you."

"My number's on the paper."

"And I'll take these away."

He drove me to a main road and left me.

The address checked out as the home of a Mr Franklin Smythe. Further checks revealed he was a widower, wife of the name of Katherine. He was an accountant, with little else to hide.

The photographs he'd given me hadn't been tampered with in any way, and the burden of proof against Pike and sons certainly seemed to suggest they were coining in an awful lot of cash for a funeral parlour. They had to be up to something.

I needed to meet Mr Pike, and fast.

X

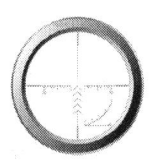

When I phoned the parlour, a suave and unctuous voice answered.

"Mr Pike?"

"Speaking."

"I believe there is some business you can help me with."

"Oh yes?"

"Me and some like-minded colleagues, if you take my meaning."

"Colleagues?"

"Yes, we have a mutual friend. I trust that you are discreet as a funeral director."

"I understand entirely," he said. "Discretion is critical in this line of work. Can we arrange for you to come here and discuss your needs, all in the strictest confidence?"

I made an appointment for noon the following day in the name of Steele.

I was conducted into a tastefully decorated funeral parlour, neutral colours, pastels, a lot of cushions and tranquil images. Music played so softly it sounded like it was coming from another room.

Pike was a burly good-looking man in his sixties. His grey hair was still thick and he had a soft, resonant voice.

He conducted me into a room at the back.

Two sofas flanked the walls. A golden light created a calming atmosphere.

"Please, sit down," he said.

He waited for me to open proceedings, before adding:

"Please be assured, we are talking quite confidentially."

"Okay," I said, feigning embarrassment and looking down at the floor.

"Have we suffered a decease recently, Mr Steele?"

"What I have come to speak to you about relates to the deceased, or rather the lack of availability, for…"

I allowed my voice to trail away and shuffled my feet, prompting him to talk.

"I think I understand."

"I have heard that you run a multifaceted business here."

"Oh yes," he said, smiling. "There are many strings to our bow. Look, why don't you take the plunge and say what it is we can help you with? You won't be disappointed."

"Romantic, or, shall I say, sexual predilections, are often strange but usually don't involve hurting other people."

I was trying to be as vague as possible while casting enough hints to get a hook into him.

"Of course."

"And, if someone is dead, what can they know of what is happening to them?"

"Indeed, that is why many people prefer cremation."

For a minute I thought I was losing him.

"The word necro has a lot of uses, and is after all only a prefix," I said.

He leaned forward.

"Let us go into the back," he said.

To the rear of the building was a remote office, jam-packed with files, ledgers, papers and directories.

"This is an unusual route. You have not come through the usual network."

Smythe had supplied a couple of names connected to the necro ring. One of them had recently died. In dropping his name I saw Pike relax.

He nodded.

"Of course. You knew him. I needed to be sure."

"So, can you help me?"

"Are you interested in male or female?"

"Both."

"For yourself or a group?"

"A group."

"I will need to meet them."

"Of course."

"We have at present a woman, fairly attractive, large breasts, recently deceased, so there are no dangers of cracking while the act is performed, and a young man in his twenties."

"Good."

"Or next week, an old lady, apparently a virgin, which is very popular, and a middle aged man."

"Will they be intact?"

"Oh yes, but you only have a few days, you understand."

I figured he stressed this because then he sold the organs and no one would want to fuck them after that.

"Who will you and your friends want?"

"The old lady and the middle aged man."

"Very well, then. I need to meet your colleagues before we arrange anything."

"I'll get in touch."

"Only speak to me," he said, handing me a card. "This is my direct line."

"I'm glad I came. I can see you are a consummate professional."

"Oh, I've been doing this for years," he said with a smile that made me want to cringe.

I left feeling like I needed to rinse my mouth out. There was a smell in the parlour that stuck in your throat.

I went into a pub on my way back and ordered a double whisky. Then I went over what I knew.

Scythe's analysis of Pike's accounts was pretty comprehensive. It would appear that he had acted as his accountant in the past. The books didn't add up, and there was certainly another line of income behind the transparent one.

I didn't believe that the necrophiliac aspect of it could be enough to create such a level of wealth, so I figured that he was doing everything Smythe had accused him of at our first meeting. He'd given me enough. I didn't need to dig into the organ scam as well.

By going for the second group of corpses I'd bought myself enough time to carry out the hit as well as saving myself from having to meet the guy again.

I rang Smythe that evening.

"The job's on. I need half up front."

"Excellent, excellent!" he said. "I can get it for you in two days."

"Fine."

"I will call you then."

The guy sounded elated.

I started planning the hit.

***

From what I could gather, Pike's son, Mervyn worked with him and was involved in all aspects of the business. Albert Pike had fathered two boys by wife Mildred, deceased, buried through Pike and sons, and the youngest one, Wilfred, was the black sheep of the family.

Albert had set up the business and name before they were born, and when he found out Wilfred was more into gambling and fast women effectively cut him out of his will.

Mervyn was moulded in his father's image, and even looked like him. He'd worshipped him from a small boy and did everything he told him.

Smythe had given me enough information to show that Pike himself was not averse to a little corpse fucking. Interestingly, Mildred had keeled over from a massive heart attack while visiting the parlour one day. Apparently, she'd gone into one of the embalming rooms and seen something.

Albert had inducted Mervyn, when of suitable age, into the sexual perks of the business and they worked side by side, employing only a part-time secretary and a team of pall-bearers who had little to do with the parlour.

I wanted to avoid a second meeting with Pike, so I conducted my surveillance at his house, a large bookmaker's place in St John's Wood. He worked hard and was rarely there, which helped me ascertain the best method of entry.

I'm good at disabling alarm systems and security. On one visit, I found a back window open. Climbing in easily, I inspected the premises for its vulnerability to a hit.

It was a comfortable house, decorated in terrible taste. Thick shag piles cushioned every room, and Pike had some odd tastes. He loved cheap oil paintings, the kind you find lining Piccadilly Circus. He also loved four bar electric fires. In addition to the central heating, there was an electric heater in most of the rooms.

A couple of locks at the back were loose and would be easy to force on a return visit. I just needed him there on his own. Mervyn lived with him, but was often out in the evenings.

Smythe delivered the thirty thousand as arranged, glowing with excitement at the prospect of his enemy's demise.

"May I ask," he asked. "How you are planning to do it?"

"I'll tell you when it's done."

He let me get on with the job.

I received a call from Pike while I prepared his hit. He was obviously keen to get me and my group of associates, as he put it, lined up for the next corpses.

"Would next Wednesday be suitable for us all to meet? We can make introductions to the goods then, if you so wish."

"Sounds good to me," I said, knowing he would be dead by then.

"Very well then, shall we say eight o'clock?"

"We'll see you then."

***

I had almost everything I needed. I knew Mervyn went to the gym late on Tuesday and decided that was the day.
Pike was in the habit of sampling the goods first. Every time a corpse came in that he wanted to offer for sale prior to dismemberment and further asset stripping, he would stay late at the parlour and try it out. He would then return home and luxuriate in a long bath. He had an account with

a company that sold bath products, oils, aromatherapy.

That Tuesday he took in two new corpses and stayed late at the parlour. A couple of candles flickered at the embalming room window.

He finally left at eight o'clock. I followed him home, where, from the back garden, I watched as the bathroom light went on almost immediately. Mervyn was at the gym. I'd seen him enter there at seven, just about the time when his father had been limbering up for his sexual kicks. He was in the habit of working out for an hour, then going out to dinner with friends. He wouldn't be back before ten.

After a couple of minutes I walked round to the side window and easily forced it with a crow bar.

It was small, but I managed to squeeze in.

Standing on a plastic bag, I slipped into the rubber soled deck shoes I'd bought for the occasion. Then I crept upstairs.

Pike was in the bath singing *My Way*, and I could smell the oils from the landing. Sneaking into the bedroom, I grabbed the electric heater he kept in there and plugged it into the extension cable in the hall. I then waited for it to heat up.

Pike was thrashing about like a sperm whale. I could make out a huge gut floating in a sea of bubbles and scum. Occasionally, he let out a rumble of bubbles.

I waited until the heater was good and hot and then walked in just as he warbled *Regrets, I've had a few*.

He was always going to see me.

But then again, too few too mention.

He let out a small high-pitched scream and emptied his bowels into the bath.

His mouth opened in mute horror, his eyes, two little balls of intense fear, as I dropped the heater in the water.

He sizzled and screamed, writhing around clutching at the sides of the bath and slipping in his own shit which was frying in the oils and sweat. The electric shock lasted long enough to put his heart out of action, and finally he slumped under the water without moving.

The room smelt of a burning turd in a perfume factory.

I watched him sink beneath the water and then left.

***

Smythe couldn't contain his joy when I told him it was done.

He arranged to meet me in his car the next day with the rest of the money.

He turned up on time and drove to a quiet road where I checked the money. It was all there, thirty thousand in cash.

I handed him back the files.

"There is just one thing," he said.

"Yes?"

"You said you would let me know how he died."

"Electrocuted in the bath."

"Oh good, very fitting," he said, then shook my hand warmly.

The last I saw of him he was beaming from ear to ear. He waved at me as he pulled the car away, disappearing into the London night, a strange interlude before a black chapter.

The Arms Dealer

XI

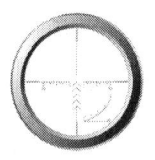

I changed address more often than my gun.

Mobility gave me security.

I became more used to hotel rooms than any trappings of home life. Now I can see it's too late for me. All that's gone away, in a fog of hits and contracts. And the big players put out a line for me. It splashed unheard in the silent waters in which I moved, circled by sharks.

Then, one day, I received the call that would change my life forever.

"Hello Jack?" said a muffled voice.

I knew instantly the caller was using a voice changer.

"Who wants to know?"

"Stuart Morris."

"How did you get my number?"

"You have a reputation."

"What do you want?"

"Can we meet?"

I thought for a moment.

"Six o'clock opposite Gloucester Road tube station."

"How will you recognise me?"

"I'll find you."

I hung up.

There was something I instinctively mistrusted

about the caller.

I spotted him on the corner, a nervous guy in grey who had bureaucrat written all over him.

"You got here early," I said.

"Jack?"

"Let's go for a drive."

He was hiding something, but that wasn't unusual, most of the people who hired me were either using me in some way or paranoid about revealing their true identities.

I parked in a quiet street and started to quiz him.

"So, what's the job?"

"My client," he said, hesitating, "is a wealthy man, and has asked me to act as his go-between."

That could go some way toward explaining his edginess. Embittered bureaucrat doing a favour for a wealthy friend, wants some cash, scared of what he's getting into.

"I've heard you have a reputation for carrying out clean and efficient jobs, and we need the very best on this. Have you heard of Global Nexus?"

"No. Should I?"

"Not at all. It's a company, or the arm of a larger one."

"Business?"

"Arms dealing."

"Okay."

"One of the directors, Kurt Spengler, has pulled off some of the biggest, most audacious arms deals of the last decade."

"So?"

"Bear with me. He has a genuine business pedigree, Harvard graduate, economist, and is a first-class businessman."

"He just got greedy."

"Oh, more than that. My client has been involved in certain business transactions with Spengler and recently came off very much the worst."

"Sorry, I don't do business grudges."

"You don't understand."

"Well, cut to the chase."

"Spengler hasn't just ripped my client off, but has taken on something that could jeopardise all of us."

He paused. He was sizing me up.

"I'm still not getting this. I need you to give me more information."

"He's planning to sell enriched plutonium to a rogue State."

"Which one?"

"Syria."

He had my attention now.

"You want Spengler taken out?"

"We need his right hand man taken out, before the deal goes through. This is in its critical stages and Syria can still be stopped. And we need some information."

"Who is he?"

"Sam Clarkson."

The name meant nothing to me.

"Background?"

"Ex-SAS. Mercenary. Skilled with weapons, martial arts expert, very dangerous."

"That it?"

"He enjoys killing and has a penchant for beating up prostitutes."

"And the information?"

"We need you to find out the trade routes they have been using and are planning to use."

"Every time you open your mouth, this gets more complicated."

"Once you've done that and terminated Clarkson, we need you to download a virus onto Global Nexus' software."

"How much are you offering?"

"A million."

That eclipsed all previous sums.

"Two," I said.

He looked startled.

"I assure you Jack, a million is a very generous offer. I have researched my figures and -."

"Two or you get someone else," I said, making to turn on the ignition.

"Shall we say one and a half?"

I weighed him up. The money was there, but I didn't want to push it.

"On two conditions."

"Yes?"

"One. You give me access to every piece of information I ask for, no hedging, no guessing games. You want this job to go smoothly, you want Clarkson taken out and no one investigating you, you give me transparency. Understood?" He nodded. "Two, I want you to supply me with whatever I need."

"It's a deal," he said, extending his hand.

"It's obvious your client is well connected."

"My client can pull a lot of strings, and I can help you navigate the sticky parts of this job. You don't need to know anything else about him."

I did.

"I'll give you a list of what I need. Also, all expenses to be charged to a credit card you give me at the outset, that covers hotels and any extras."

"Would a budget of, say, £100,000 be enough?"

"It depends on how long this takes." He was

jotting this down. "I will call you tomorrow and arrange a meeting, and I want half up front and the expense account."

He wrote a mobile number down on a piece of paper and I dropped him outside Gloucester Road tube station. I drove away, thinking this is the job I could retire on.

The line was coiling up like a noose.

XII

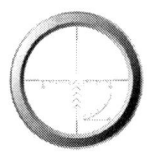

He met me the next day with a case full of cash. The money was all there, and I knew we were talking serious business.

He'd booked a room at the Savoy.

I spent less than an hour with him before leaving with the information I needed and a platinum credit card in the name of Lewis Carmichael.

I spent the next two days familiarising myself with the backgrounds of Spengler and Clarkson.

What Morris had told me panned out. Global Nexus was certainly dealing in arms in a big way, selling masses of weapons and laundering the money through sister companies and asset-striping. It owned a small property empire and its turnover was several billion a year.

Clarkson was a real charmer with a string of scalps on his belt. A trained marksman, he'd made a name for himself in the Gulf and was expert in the use of biological weapons.

He would be my hardest hit to date.

***

The premises of Global Nexus were a glass fronted block of offices near Blackfriars.

There was a secretive air to the building which was

evident when you walked in.

Spengler was a large man with a booming voice who communicated through orders and questions.

He would harangue his staff over what he viewed as failings, but rarely fired anyone, since he was content with what they were doing and liked to keep people on their toes by injecting them with doses of insecurity at regular intervals.

Clarkson didn't work at Global Nexus. He was employed by Spengler to travel where the business was, set up and oversee deals, and occasionally kill people.

The files Morris had given me detailed transactions as far back as several years ago, and it was clear that the arms dealing had accelerated in intensity.

To all intents and purposes, the main business was weapons. Anything else was a cover-up.

There were over a hundred staff on board and excluding secretaries and finance, the key players were hard-nosed business negotiators who had to know exactly what Spengler was involved in. You can only keep so many employees in the dark.

He had a couple of right-hand men with military backgrounds and operated from a closed circle, favouring secrecy.

The building blended in perfectly with the financial landscape and drew little attention. Exactly what Spengler wanted.

I had to get to see Clarkson, which was not going to be easy.

He rarely visited the offices, so I needed to pursue another route.

That is how I became an arms dealer.

***

I travelled to Dubai with business contacts set up by Morris and his associates.

The ease with which I found myself taken into confidential circles immediately made me suspicious that I was dealing with a client who was highly connected in government circles.

I mixed on the circuit for weeks, moving from the intense heat to the iced air-conditioning and the cold and seedy company of international arms dealers. Guys with greed etched into their DNA with battery acid.

And one afternoon, I made the contact I needed.

"Haven't seen you before on the circuit," a smug English businessman said, extending a limp hand, "Charles Sinclair."

"Lewis Carmichael."

"Selling or buying?"

"Both. Except I'm finding what's on offer here is pretty tried and tested, if you take my meaning."

"Oh yes?"

"I'm looking for something a little different."

"Something not officially on the agenda?"

"Definitely."

"Look. Here's my card. Why don't we meet later?"

I watched him disappear and went through the motions for the rest of the day.

Later at the hotel I rang him.

"Carmichael. You're interested in something else aren't you?"

"I am."

"Meet me at *Le Meridien*, say, seven tonight?"

I phoned Morris for a background check and he got back to me an hour later.

Sinclair was an ex-property dealer who'd done

some shady deals and pissed a lot of people off to all accounts. He'd been into arms dealing for a few years now, hiding it as part of an otherwise above board business.

He was wanted by the Inland Revenue.

Morris sounded pleased. "He's a good find. He's dealt with Clarkson before and the two of them are apparently about to engage in something big."

I met Sinclair at his hotel and endured half an hour of his self-congratulatory drivel.

"There are a lot of small-time operators in this business, if you're not one of them, then we're talking business," he said.

"I'm not."

"How much can you put up?"

"Two hundred mill."

He blinked, disguising his surprise by gulping his drink.

"Excellent. Then, I have someone I want you to meet. Sam Clarkson. He's in this with me and we need a couple more people on board."

"Never heard of him."

"No reason you should have."

"What exactly are we talking about?"

"I can tell you're a player. Nuclear weapons."

"Good."

"Who is your client?"

"A government."

"Sounds a bit cagey to me."

"I'll tell you more when I meet your contact."

"He's a player, don't worry."

"I never worry," I said.

We arranged a meeting for two days' time, and I planned my part carefully.

***

I first met Sam Clarkson at Sinclair's hotel.

He was late, and after an hour of enduring Sinclair's self-praise, I was relieved when I heard a tap at the door.

He walked in with the slow, measured pace and stiff bearing of a man who had spent too long in the army. Combat was etched into his gait, and he gripped me with a strong handshake which I met. Two animals who knew each other's scent.

"You Army?" he said.

"Nah, Royal Marines."

"Regiment?"

"Nope. Like I said. Royal Marines."

He nodded. "I knew a couple of ex Royal Marines. Good operators."

"And you?"

"Paras for a bit, then went on to something else."

"Sounds like you've seen a fair bit of action."

He narrowed his eyes at me. "More than most."

"Drink, Sam?" Sinclair said.

"Whisky."

"Lewis?"

"Same for me."

"I know I'm always in good company with Army men," he said, pouring them. "It's the training. Second to none."

"Some units are better than others," Clarkson said.

I watched as he removed his jacket and sat on the sofa opposite me.

He had that wiry, deeply muscled frame that comes with years of army training. Not the bulk of someone who pushes weights, but someone who is trained for combat.

He sat back and sipped his whisky, taking me in.

Finally, Sinclair broke the silence.

"Lewis is interested in buying into our latest venture."

Clarkson continued to watch me.

"How did you hear about us?"

"We met at last week's conference."

He gave me a look that said he didn't buy it.

I was going to have to convince him I was seriously on board and that would take time.

"I've been dealing for a client for a while now."

"Haven't we all?"

"Look, we can all sit here and play the game of mistrust, at the end of the day I don't know either of you from Adam. I suggest we talk business, you show me what you've got, and I'll let the money do the talking."

Sinclair looked relieved.

"Now that's my kind of language."

"Okay. Say we do business with you," Clarkson said, "What's in it for us?"

"My client's money, and this is only the first of many deals he's interested in. We can give you a sizeable amount up front, financing for future ventures, and you get another guy on board with military training."

"How much up front?"

"I'll have to check, but this is what I propose. We meet next week with your plan in place, so I can look it over and get approval, and I give you some initial backing. If you decide you don't want to deal, then that's fine, I can take my business elsewhere."

"Why us then?"

"You seem like serious players to me, and that's what I'm looking for."

Sinclair raised his glass.

"I'll drink to that."

"How much have you been told?" Clarkson said.

"Just that you're about to sell some nuclear weapons to an interested third party."

"That's all?"

"That's it."

"That's all you need to know for the moment."

I have one question."

Clarkson leaned forward.

"What?"

"What protection do you have?"

"In the way of?"

"Back-up."

"Fire power?"

"Yes."

"Enough. When we meet next and if this deal goes ahead with you on board, then I'll tell you more."

"Trust us," Sinclair said.

It was obvious who was running this show.

I left after another drink and phoned Morris back at my hotel so he could start organising the finances.

XIII

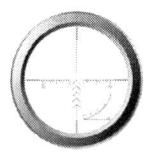

I knew Clarkson wasn't going to be easy. He was suspicious of everyone.

I told Morris to put out some phoney background on me that would convince him to do business. He played his part well and I became the man Clarkson was looking for, with all the credentials that would hook him in.

"I've put together a package saying you're ex-military and have been working for the US and British government," he said when he called me back. "Clarkson will have to hunt for the information, as he would expect, but he'll find it. And he'll see you as a fellow mercenary he can manipulate."

"And the money?"

"We've opened an account showing ten mill in it."

"I hope that's enough."

It would get me in with Clarkson and in the meantime I would smoke Morris out.

I knew all along he was working for the government. There was no way he could have put that package together without being an agent. Every time he got back to me with what I wanted I saw a little more. What I couldn't see was the puppet master's face.

I knew the government game was use and dispose: guys in my position eventually walked the plank toward a ticking bomb. I figured I could do the job and get out.

Meanwhile, someone was bloodying the waters with shark bait.

When the call came, it was from Sinclair.

"We're thinking tomorrow, about noon."

"Fine."

"At your hotel."

"I'm staying at the Al Murooj."

The next day they turned up together.

I showed them into the sitting room and after serving drinks got down to business.

"I've arranged my part. Are we playing?"

"We've checked you out, and you seem to be telling the truth," Clarkson said.

He looked more relaxed than the last time.

"You said something about arranging finances," Sinclair said.

"It's all here."

I put the folder down on the coffee table.

Clarkson picked it up.

He looked through it in silence then passed it to Sinclair.

After a few minutes, he closed it and said, "Looks good to me."

"We need more money," Clarkson said.

"I know, I can arrange that for you."

"Fine. Then we're on. Charles?"

"Yes. Absolutely."

"Okay. Now you tell me more about the deal."

Clarkson stood up. "We've been doing some trade with Syria. The people we're dealing with…"

"Who are?"

"Syrian military. The government's elite corps. They're interested in buying into the nuclear arms race. We have enriched plutonium coming into Libya via Australia.

We need you to come out to Libya with us, and then on to the sales point which will be in Damascus. Any problems?"

"None."

Sinclair leaned forward.

"This is a very delicate operation, Lewis. We need to make sure nothing goes wrong, which is why the fact that you're ex-military has swung things in your favour."

"How is that going to help?"

"Things might get tough at the borders."

"You're transporting it across?"

"Yes."

"There are factions, groups with their own interests who could endanger the project, some of them bandits," Clarkson said. "We envisage the possibility of shoot-outs and we will arm you."

"Charles has no background, isn't that a little risky?"

"Charles won't be in on the transport. I need another guy on board who can handle himself, which is why we're interested in you."

"I'll be at Damascus conducting the negotiations, and wait for you to turn up," Sinclair said.

"I get the picture."

"We'll meet again to talk through the plans. There will be two stages."

"Which are?"

"Delivery of the plutonium, then the other components."

"What weapons will we be carrying?"

"Just let me take care of that."

I decided to let it go.

"Then we're on," Sinclair said, standing up.

After a few more drinks they left and I relayed the information through to Morris.

The best way to play Clarkson was to let him feel he was in control.

    I had a plan as to how to get his trust and it would take effect at the border.

***

Everything went smoothly. Until we reached the crossing.

    Clarkson and I had flown out to Libya, passed a night in a hotel talking through the next day's movements and spoken to Sinclair, who said everything was okay at his end. We'd checked the transport and he'd armed me with a *Sig Sauer* pistol.

    The next day we received and checked the plutonium, connected the transporter to the juggernaut and drove off.

    Once we got to the border, we were quizzed for a long time by the guards.

    The ID they'd arranged worked and we got through, but hit a dead end when we came across an overturned tree in one of the roads.

    It was too narrow to turn, so we set about shifting it.

    As we did, we heard shots over our heads.

    Clarkson dived for cover, and I got into the juggernaut.

    I let him fire out a few rounds from behind some trees before moving in and taking out two of the guys with the SIG.

    He was impressed.

    "You're good," he said. "Better than a lot of the guys I used to work with."

    "I like to think I've still got it."

    "I owe you one."

"I told you I can handle myself."

He stretched out his hand. His grip was firm, but more relaxed now.

"Okay, how about moving the tree?" I said.

We arrived that evening and parked the goods in the lock-up before heading to the hotel.

We had something to eat then discussed the plans for the next day before retiring for the night.

Back in my room I called Morris on my mobile.

"You're in Damascus?"

"Yes. And the guys you put in the hills did a good job. Fired just close enough to convince him, backing off when I came out."

"I told you we wouldn't let you down."

"The tree was a nice touch."

"So you have his trust now?"

"Think so. Close enough to find out what we need."

XIV

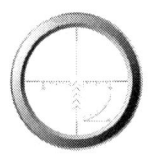

As it turned out, Clarkson was not the only person I was to rescue.

Lauren Smiles was Spengler's personal secretary. He employed hundreds of them, but used her as his PA because of her languages and people skills. She had a way of putting people at their ease. She inspired confidence, a useful commodity to the tricksters who paid her salary.

Spengler treated her badly, paid her as little as he could get away with, and backed off from touching her up, having had his face slapped, but made endless sexist jokes about her when she was out of the room.

He shuttled her around on business, never consulting her, and used her as his general dog's body.

It was at the offices of Global Nexus in Damascus that I first met her.

They were trading under the name of United Investments, but it was just an outpost of Global.

Clarkson had asked me to come to a meeting at the offices to look over some paperwork relating to future investments in the deal.

Lauren greeted me at reception. She had a pleasant manner and a warm voice and there was something about her that made her stand out from the crowd.

"He's not here yet, can I get you a coffee?" she said.

"That would be nice."

She was neatly dressed in a designer suit which hugged her figure.

Her manner immediately put me at ease.

"Would you like to wait in the office, Mr Carmichael?"

"This is fine."

There was a sofa in the reception area and I sat down as she returned to her desk.

She seemed to be the only employee working there and the offices had an isolated feel about them.

I listened as she took various phone calls, noting how unflappable and calm she was. She had something about her, some allure I couldn't put my finger on. I also realised as I sat there she was someone I didn't come across too often in my line of work: an honest, professional woman unpolluted by crime.

She was almost lulling me into a relaxation I consider dangerous to my need for alertness.

I decided on conversation as an antidote.

"So, how long have you been working here?"

"Well I don't, Mr Carmichael."

"Please call me Lawrence."

"I work in London, Lawrence, at Global Nexus's head office, but Mr Spengler sends me out here from time to time."

"I see."

"It's hard work, but I enjoy the variety."

Behind her professional charm I detected strain: an uneasiness.

"Is he a good boss?"

She looked at me for an instant and said, "I've got no complaints."

"Well, I'll be doing some work with Sam Clarkson,

so we may well meet again."

I saw her look away when I mentioned his name.

"You'll see me more likely in London. What do you do?"

Just then the phone rang, and Clarkson walked in.

I was ushered into the office, where we went over the brief.

They were outlaying a billion on this project, intending to rake back ten times more.

It had been immaculately planned out and I was definitely riding in on the crest of a wave and could blow this thing sky high.

Clarkson's mobile went and he left me alone for a few minutes. While he was gone I downloaded a lot of information from the computer onto a memory stick.

When I left, Lauren was still on the phone. I waved at her and left the building.

***

Once we'd delivered the plutonium over at the outpost, we returned to London.

The last stage had been easy, no hold-ups, no checks, and I suspected that Global had a major insider in the Syrian government who was controlling all the movements. These were definitely top names. Self-protection and secrecy surrounded every level of the operation like a barbed wire fence.

From London to Damascus a miasma of lies choked the truth out of the situation like a still-born baby.

We had a de-brief at Clarkson's hotel, then parted for a few weeks before stage two.

I'd got quite a lot from the stick, trade routes and financial figures, some other business deals and a lot of personnel information, but there was a whole lot more.

I passed on everything I'd gathered to Morris.

He had one question:

"When's the hit?"

"I can't tell you. When I've got what you need and I can exit safely."

I needed to corner Clarkson, but there was a lot to do before that happened. Also, I wanted to find out more about exactly what I was involved in.

Although he was less wary of me after the shoot-out, he continued to be suspicious and closed. Habit of a lifetime serving in the army and killing, I guess.

The second stage of the deal was to deliver parts for the plutonium enrichment programme the Syrians were planning.

They'd constructed huge underground factories, where workers, some of the Syrian, many defectors from the Soviet Union or smuggled out of North Korea, laboured in anonymity and un-spendable wealth.

I never went down there, only Clarkson did that, but it was surplus to my needs.

I kept reminding myself of the two things I needed to do: get the information and take Clarkson out, after which I planned to retire. That was about as easy as crossing a minefield for a loaf of bread.

The personnel information I'd downloaded made interesting reading: complaint after complaint by disgruntled employees. Spengler had worked his way through a long list of PAs, all with top professional credentials.

All of them had left to get jobs elsewhere, often for less pay.

Checking through Lauren Smiles' pedigree was educational: she was highly employable. Also, she'd taken out an official grievance procedure against a member of staff whose name was classified, alleging sexual harassment. It had been resolved via a pay rise. She seemed too good for the job.

The word classified appeared several times: there were a lot of female staff who'd complained of being left alone in offices where incidents of sexual harassment had occurred, while the perpetrator was never identified.

One even went to the police with a rape allegation. The CPS never prosecuted.

Still, what did Spengler care for the workers? If his right hand man liked rough sex, he'd just add a fat tip.

We flew back out a month later and stopped off in another border town hotel. Sinclair as usual was dealing with things at the Damascus end.

Clarkson informed me that we would need to take another route this time.

"After what happened last time, I've found another way round."

The parts arrived on schedule and we drove through the night on deserted roads, taking it in turns.

No danger presented itself, and even the security guards sleepily waved us through.

We delivered the goods and left.

Then came the series of protracted negotiations where we had to ensure adequate funds were cleared.

That was when the funds had to be certified, and was always the part of the plan that worried me the most. Morris was not going to risk parting with that amount of money, so the figures were all smoke and mirrors.

Clarkson left me alone in the offices of United Investments for a couple of hours while he went to take care of a couple of things.

It was my second meeting with Lauren.

She looked different, worn out somehow.

"See you're still stuck out here," I said. "I thought you'd be back in London by now."

"Too much to do."

Compared to the first meeting she seemed strangely uncommunicative and I tried again.

"Work getting you down?"

"You could say that."

She was feeding reams of paper into the photocopier. I walked over to the water cooler and as she turned I noticed a livid bruise just under her left eye. It was heavily made-up, and had I been standing any further away I wouldn't have noticed it.

She stopped.

"Has someone hit you?"

She turned her head.

"It's nothing."

"No it's not. Someone's punched you, Lauren."

Behind the professional persona were stifled tears. An isolated employee who I could see wanted to talk.

"Who was it?"

Her eyes were brimming now.

"I've just had enough," she said. "If it wasn't for the money, I'd quit tomorrow. That bastard-."

"Who? Spengler?"

"No. Clarkson, your business colleague."

"What happened?"

She sat down.

"I don't know if I should be talking about this. What the hell? Last week I was working late, as usual, and he comes in. Drunk." I didn't know he'd been back to Damascus since our last visit. "He starts saying how beautiful I am and can he take me out for a meal. Look, he's really not my type. I'm a professional woman, do this job, and try to have a life."

"Sure."

"Well, he starts making innuendos. I bet you're a bit of a goer, that sort of thing. Have you ever fucked a squaddy before? I just ignored him, and then as I'm making to leave, he grabs one of my boobs."

"No one else around?"

"No. I slapped him as hard as I could. He punched out instantly and that's how I got this."

"Squaddies, eh?"

"Yeah, well, it didn't end there. He pushed me up against the wall, put his hand up my skirt and started feeling me up. I started screaming at the top of my lungs and although the building was empty, it unnerved him."

"You shouldn't be put in that kind of position."

"Tell me about it. All the people Spengler sends for me to deal with are scum, right bastards, present company excepted."

"Thanks."

"No, really. There's something different about you."

"Nice to know."

"Look, I'm a professional woman, but this job's been getting me down for years. Staff are not treated correctly. People are frightened. Clarkson's been hassling me for months. He's got a reputation. And as far as a grievance procedure is concerned at this company, money is seen as a fix for everything. I'd quit tomorrow if I could."

"What's stopping you?"

"I don't have time to look for anything else."

The phone went and a few minutes later Clarkson came back. I suggested going to my hotel to finish the meeting.

He asked why.

"I'm not sure. I think that secretary's ear wigging us."

"Her! I can believe that. She's a real little tart, fucked just about everyone in Global. I don't trust her. I want her out of the way."

***

In all the hits I'd carried out for Martoni and privately there were zero opportunities for casualties. Mixing in the legitimised world of businessmen and secret services I saw how careless they were with incidental damage: staff and passers-by were all part of the area of fair risk as far as they were concerned.

They hid behind their shield of legitimacy like thieves in a security van. Interestingly, the Mafia minimised that kind of risk. And I didn't do collateral damage.

XV

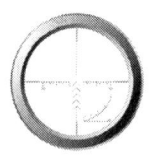

The next morning I turned up at the offices of United Investments bright and early.

I'd been doing some thinking which was not strictly part of my remit, but I was getting sick of the sound of Morris's voice and the sight of Clarkson's narrow eyes. I'd started to want something more than this and I'd known it for some time.

I knew Lauren was at risk and I didn't like the sight of casualties.

She was working on her own and let me in.

"He's not here," she said. "I'm not expecting him, either."

"I haven't come to see him."

"Oh?"

"You know what you were saying yesterday?" She looked blankly at me. "About wanting to quit?"

"Oh that."

"Well I might just be able to help."

"How?"

"You want to leave?"

She hesitated for a moment.

"I'd walk tomorrow if I could find something better."

"Then I think I have a job for you. Here's my number. I want you to call me if anything else happens."

"Like what?"
"Like that bruise."
She looked worried.
"All right, but …"
"Can I have a number to call you on?"
"This is confidential."
"Strictly between us."
She scribbled it on a piece of paper and I left.
The clock was ticking.
Back at my hotel I called Clarkson.
"The money'll be through within twenty-four hours," I said.
"Good. About time. We need to meet again."
"I'll come round to your hotel tomorrow at one."
I hung up and dialled Morris.
"We're nearly there. I need something from you."
"What?"
"A job for a woman called Lauren Smiles."
"This isn't an employment agency," he said.
"Look, this is more complicated than you let on. There is a totally innocent party caught up in this, a woman's life is at risk. Does the British government sacrifice its own that easily?"
There was long pause as he reflected on the implication of what I'd said.
"Government?"
"Look, I don't care who you're working for, but I know a spook when I see one."
"Who I represent is not the issue. We've paid you to-."
"I am not in the habit of watching innocent people get caught up in crossfire. This situation is far more complex than you've let on. If you want me to carry out the remit, you do this. The money's barely enough to guarantee

success."

There was silence at the other end.

"Who is she?"

"Works for Spengler. She's going to get killed if I don't get her out of here. Are you spooks less moral than a hitman?"

"What does she do?"

"PA. She needs to be placed by the end of the month in a job paying at least 150K. You have her details. I need confirmation and all the paperwork fast."

I figured the 150K would please her.

***

I spent the next day talking through the final details of the plan with Clarkson. He wanted the money through and I just wanted him dead.

We were putting the finishing touches on the deal and I wanted him relaxed for the hit.

The last thing I needed was a suspicious mercenary on the prowl.

I thought he looked a little edgy when I left, like his mind was on something else.

I went back to my hotel and told Morris I was ready for the hit.

"Good."

"Have you sorted out the job?"

"It's done. I'll e-mail the details through."

"Include a contract."

I wanted to have something solid to present to her.

A few hours later the phone went.

A voice I hardly recognised just said my name. Then silence.

"Yes?"

"It's Lauren."

"Is everything okay?"

"No. Could you come? I'm at the office."

I went straight there and found her nursing a bleeding nose. Her tights were torn and she was shaking.

I took her back to her hotel, gave her a brandy and heard how Clarkson had gone there as she was finishing for the day and tried to rape her.

"If it hadn't been for these," she said, pointing at her heels, "He'd have done it. I kicked him hard enough to knock his balls off and I hope I did."

"You're in a totally unacceptable position as an employee of a very wealthy company, Lauren. This can't carry on."

"I know. I don't want to go back there."

She started to shake again.

"Maybe you don't have to."

She didn't really register my last comment.

I made sure she was okay. She was tough. Apart from a few bruises and a bloody nose, nothing broken. But I wanted her out of there.

I'd never forgotten the sight of some innocent bystanders blown apart by an errant army bomb. Shopping and school satchels lay scattered among the debris. Tissue fragments and limbs lay useless as sweet wrappers, heads rocked to stasis in pools of blood. I was going to make sure I only had one memory like that.

I left her to sleep and said I'd call in the morning.

Back at my hotel, I rang Morris.

"One more thing."

"What now?"

"I need two tickets out of here for four tomorrow."

"Let me guess, names of Carmichael and Smiles."
"That's right."
"Travelling together?"
"You got it."

***

The next morning I packed my bags and called Lauren.

Her voice was croaky.

"This is early."

My watch said seven o'clock.

"I need you to go to the office now. I'll meet you there in an hour."

"Look, what is going on?"

"I'll tell you everything when I see you."

Reluctantly, she agreed.

I got there just before her.

She looked tired and was still shaking. The makeup was heavier.

"I hope this is good, Lawrence."

"It is. I need to use your computer."

She showed me into the office where Clarkson and I had conducted our business and I downloaded what Morris had sent.

It was all there, a job contract with good perks with a city company, starting date, two weeks' time. All Lauren needed to do was sign.

She sat there for a while taking it in, then looked around the room and said:

"Is this for real?"

"Totally."

I could see she was still in shock.

"150K? The job sounds amazing."

"All you need to do is to accept the offer."

"I don't feel comfortable leaving like this."

"You could take Global to a tribunal. Do you want to find yourself in another situation like last night? What's it going to be next? He'll try again. Your boss has no concern for your well-being, Lauren." She looked at the contract again. "This is not a situation you want to be involved with any more."

"No. I don't. Easy as that? And I'm in another job?"

"Easy as that. People pay good money for your skills, and treat you right."

"I don't know how you've arranged this."

"Let's just say I have a wide experience of recruitment."

I could see her hesitating, and as she looked about the office I saw her eyes harden at the memory of what had happened to her there.

"Hand me a pen."

"I have two tickets to London for this afternoon."

"Why so quick?"

"Why wait? I know Clarkson. Do you really want to stay on here?"

"No. I could hardly bring myself to come in this morning. I have things to finish off. I'll work here until twelve."

"We leave for the airport at two-thirty. See you at your hotel."

Back at the Intercontinental I got the weapon ready. Then I went to see Clarkson.

***

At exactly one o'clock I knocked on his door.

I got there just in time.

"I've just checked the account and the money's not through," he said. "I'm beginning to doubt you."

"There's got to be a perfectly simple explanation. You know my credentials."

"I thought I did."

"Have you checked with Sinclair?"

"I'm just about to phone him."

"Look, if I was going to do a runner, I wouldn't have turned up here, would I?"

"I'm not talking about you doing a runner, Carmichael."

"Let me call my people and check."

"No. Sit down, I'm calling Spengler."

There was no more time.

As he turned his back to pick up the phone, I pulled out the knife.

I slipped it around his neck and severed the jugular first time. There was a brief moment when he reached out behind him and then pushed his hands up to his throat.

He turned round, rage and shock in his eyes. He was trying to stem the flow of blood which was spraying out from between his fingers like a shower head.

He ran into the bathroom, his shirt dripping. I knew he didn't have long.

He fumbled inside the cabinet for a gun and as he touched the metal I turned him round and stabbed him through the heart.

I left the blade in for a while before removing and cleaning it.

By the time I left he was dead.

I took the files and placed the *Do Not Disturb* sign over his door.

Then I went back to my hotel.

***

The files had almost everything I needed. Just the security numbers were missing.

I phoned Lauren.

"You said half two."

"I know. I just need something from the office."

"What?"

"Some papers I must have left there earlier."

"I can't go back. I'm packing."

"You still got your keys?"

"Yes."

"I can pick them up from you."

"Okay."

I paid my bill and left with the last of my belongings.

Dodging the traffic, I got to the offices of United Investments at two o'clock.

It didn't take me long to hack into the files and get everything I needed. I e-mailed it all through to Morris. Then I downloaded the virus onto Global Nexus's software.

I saw some interesting things they didn't want me to know about. The files contained enough data to bring the government down: a web of corruption that went right to the top. This was all about self-protection and I wasn't about to become the fall guy. I took the opportunity to e-mail it through to myself. When I'd finished I had just enough time to make our flight.

Morris called me.

He'd obviously checked his e-mails.

"Good work," he said. "The hit's complete?"

"It's done."

We made it with enough time to check in and I watched as Lauren boarded the plane that would take her to her new life.

XVI

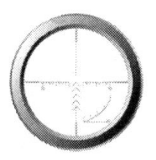

Landing back in London brought a sense of relief and also new problems.

I realised Lauren was still at risk from Spengler.

I dropped her back at her flat. It had an unlived-in feel and was fairly basic.

She looked shaky and was coming out of the daze of her shock.

"Did I mention your new boss has a couple of flats sitting empty near to the offices?"

"No."

"You'll have a long journey if you stay here."

I could see in her face she was working things out for herself.

"Are you suggesting I leave this fantastic, homey place? Can't you see how much TLC I've put into it? It's so Candy Brothers."

"Do you fancy taking a look at the flats?"

She smiled wryly.

"You going to take care of me, Lawrence?"

We had a couple of drinks and then I left.

***

The next morning I dialled Morris.

"She's still in danger, and with the job done,

they're going to come after her."

"We're not running a hotel service."

"I need you to find her a place near to her new job. She's renting, it shouldn't be hard."

There was a sigh at the other end of the line.

"I'll put someone onto it."

He called me back later that afternoon.

"I've found you two flats in central London. Affordable, I imagine, with her salary. I'll send you the details through."

"Have you checked the files I sent?"

"Yes. It's all there. We're moving on it. You did a good job."

"And my fee?"

"Will be sent through by the end of the week."

I checked my emails and knew instantly someone had been trying to hack in. But I have firewalls on firewalls.

And what it confirmed is I'd been right all along.

Right to mistrust Morris. Right to get Lauren out of there. This job was a pile of explosives sitting in a shopping mall with two guys wrestling for the switch.

Morris was waist deep in shit.

His boss, whoever he was, wanted Spengler and Clarkson out of the way because of what they had on him. But first he wanted the information taken out of circulation.

As Martoni said, data is the new gold.

Well I had the bullion staring back at me from my computer screen and it showed a story that would set the papers alight. A scoop a young journalist could retire on.

The British government was trading with the enemy to hide the national debt and someone very high up was pulling Morris's wires.

That name was missing.

The more senior secret service personnel needed investigating, but the political connections were definitely there.

Morris's own CV was disguised: he was far better placed in intelligence than the credentials the information I had showed.

I needed help, and knew it wouldn't be long before I called Martoni.

***

I took Lauren flat viewing.

She liked the second one and we put a deposit down on the spot.

She could move in immediately.

The next day I helped her pack her things up.

She was looking edgy and had been drinking.

"I'm in the middle of something aren't I?"

"Nothing I can't handle."

"This is all moving too fast."

"You really want to stay here?"

She'd obviously worked a lot out for herself, but I could sense questions lurking.

I loaded everything onto the van and moved her in myself. When I left her, she was a little drunk, and a little happier.

***

I got a call from Morris the following morning.

"Someone spotted you."

"When?"

"Leaving Clarkson's room."

I thought for a moment. There were no staff

around when I left and I'm always vigilant. I hadn't seen anyone, so if I was seen, then I must have been followed.

"Who?"

"One of Spengler's smurfs. We're looking into it. They knew Clarkson was dead minutes after you left. And you're right, they're after the girl. You were lucky to get out of there."

Either this was a cover for what he'd got planned for me, or a warning, since he still wanted me alive. Either way I wasn't going to take any risks.

If it was the second, then Clarkson must have started asking questions about me before I got there. I'd always thought the money could let me down.

I thought through my movements and realised just how much danger Lauren was in.

I called her, but got her voicemail.

"It's Lawrence. Don't go out, don't go anywhere, I'm coming straight round."

I waited outside for an hour before she turned up.

Finally I saw her at the end of the street with some shopping.

"Hello stranger."

"I've left a message for you."

"My phone's switched off. What's the problem?"

Not wanting to reveal too much, I explained that Spengler was a ruthless individual who didn't like his staff deserting him for a better job.

"That's it? Tell me something I don't know. He was a total bastard. Who cares? What can he do?"

"He's got a track record of roughing people up if they get on the wrong side of him."

"How come you know so much about him?"

"Let's just say I've been checking him out."

"Well, he's history. If he wants to take me to a

tribunal, then I'll gladly tell them about all his sexual harassments. Rape never came as part of my job description. There are a lot of female staff -."

"Have you noticed anyone hanging around?"

"Like who?"

"Someone following you."

"Only you. Look, this is getting a little bit spooky."

She was panicking.

"Don't worry about it. I'm here to help. I figured you could do with a spare set of hands."

"True."

"So, come on, what can I do?"

"Help me unpack."

I spent the rest of the day helping her settle in.

Over a glass of wine later she thanked me.

"I like the flat. And I didn't mean anything by it, by the way."

"What?"

"Only you following me. I kind of like it."

I drove away that evening knowing they wouldn't let things slide that easily.

As I was parking my phone rang. It was Morris.

"You were seen by a guy called Jonas Hinch. He works for Spengler and served in the Paras with Clarkson. They don't know who you are, but they're after you."

"And Lauren?"

"Her too."

"What are you doing about it?"

"We're keeping them under surveillance. I'll call you tomorrow with more information."

I went to bed and worried about Lauren.

XVII

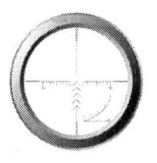

It's all about the line of communication. Military training. And if the line isn't straight, people get hurt. Orders lack transparency and suddenly you're in a shark pool, swimming through blood.

Morris called the next morning.

"We're planning something that could take Hinch and Spengler out completely. They're the only ones who know what you look like."

"And Lauren?"

"We're putting two men onto her first thing Monday morning. If anyone tries anything, they'll deal with it."

I got to her flat at twelve o'clock. She opened the door in her dressing gown.

"It's a bit early," she said.

"Thought you might need a bit more help."

"You can open a few boxes while I have a bath, if you like."

"Show me which ones."

I spent the day with her and by the end of it, her flat was looking more homely.

I wasn't going to take any chances, so I sat outside all night. Just far enough away for my car to be invisible. I saw her lights go off just before midnight.

At nine the next morning two guys turned up in a

black Ford. I phoned Morris and gave him the reg number.

"They're our men."

"Tell me if they see anything."

As I drove back I began to feel a little easier about Lauren.

I started to set a trap for Hinch.

***

I figured he would head straight for her old flat.

I had the keys, which I said I'd give to the estate agents for her.

Tuesday evening I went round there with a few beers and some food. I put all the lights on and waited.

It wasn't long before a blue Volvo pull up outside. It stopped, then drove off.

It turned at the end of the street, circled the flat, then disappeared.

Five minutes later it returned. There were two guys sitting inside. One of them was talking on his mobile.

A few minutes later, the phone rang at the flat.

"Hello?"

"Is Lauren there?"

"Who?"

"Lauren Smiles."

"Oh, you mean the last flat mate. No, this place has been re-let. She doesn't live here anymore."

"Got a number for her?"

"No sorry."

I hung up and watched as they waited outside.

I phoned Morris on my mobile and gave him the car reg and a description.

"We'll get onto it," he said.

An hour later they drove off. I waited and then

made my getaway.

***

I saw Lauren again on the Wednesday.

She called to ask for some help.

"There are a few heavy things I need lifting."

I went round there and had supper with her.

When I left, the two spooks were still outside. They were too obvious. I wondered when she would notice them, annoyed that Morris had sent a couple of monkeys.

***

The next day he called. I hadn't seen Hinch or been back to Lauren's old flat since.

I was beginning to wonder if I was going to have to carry out a double hit on this assignment, one of them unpaid.

"We've dealt with it," Morris said.

"How?"

"The car you told us about. It was back at the address you gave us. They were seen breaking in and leaving. We had them followed, and a few hours later they drove off from the location where we had them under surveillance. The car detonated. Both dead."

"Good. What about the other matters?"

"Spengler?"

"Yes."

"Ongoing."

I knew he wouldn't give up that easily, but at least one part of this was tidied up.

The British government really wanted this guy, and they were spinning me a line.

XVIII

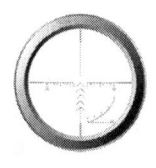

I figured it was competition.

Spengler had muscled in on deals the government wanted.

I used some of my Mafia contacts to get what information I needed.

Spengler had worked alongside the government for years, pulling off big deals.

Like all people who have their uses, he became an obstacle. Got greedy. Started setting up his own deals.

He got contracts the government wanted and built a pretty big empire.

Clarkson and Spengler were on the verge of building their own army. They obviously had plans. Spengler had bought up a lot of land with shooting rights, enclosed spaces where he could train his men. Meanwhile, Clarkson was recruiting a lot of ex-military personnel, mercenaries with a good track record of killing.

Morris had been with the secret service for decades.

Behind him was a much more shadowy figure who was proving harder to identify.

I knew there was someone powerful behind the orders and I needed to know who, if I was to feel this job was truly put to bed.

The hook they'd put out for me led right along the

line back to him, and it was his hand that was holding it.

I called Martoni and he helped out.

When he came back to me with the information I wanted, it confirmed everything I suspected.

"The man giving the orders is very well connected, very high up, Jack," he said.

"Who is it?"

"Your defense secretary, Alan Klein."

"That figures. Thank you."

I knew a puppet master had his hand up Morris' arse, and now I knew who it was.

Klein had almost lost the promotion he'd worked all his political career for because of his obsession with building up Britain's nuclear arsenal.

One of his rivals pulled out of the race unexpectedly, followed by a well-publicised sex scandal.

He saw off the opponents and toned down his rhetoric once he was in, disguising his plan amidst well-massaged and confusing economic figures. He also gave the most generous tax-breaks to Middle England for decades, which went down well, and converted his image from that of a fanatic to a benevolent uncle.

He had never stopped pursuing his goal and crossed legal lines in the pursuit of nuclear weapons.

He'd known Spengler from his time in the City, and started up business dealings with him again. Then came the crunch.

They were both after the same deals, and Klein didn't like it.

Still, they carried on dealing. Klein's greed got the better of him when Spengler approached him over Syria. He got close to Clarkson on the deal. And of course Spengler and Clarkson got to know too much about Klein.

Once he'd stashed his cash, he wanted Spengler

and Clarkson taken out of circulation. It seems the files I'd got hold of were more important than the hit. Klein wanted his reputation intact when he retired.

The money from my job came through and I banked one and a half mill.

I stashed it in the Cayman Islands and got back to work.

***

Late one Saturday night Lauren called.

"You know you asked me about noticing anyone?"

"Yes."

"Well, it may be nothing, but there are these two guys I keep seeing. I think they're following me."

"I'll come straight round."

It was almost midnight when I parked in aside road near Lauren"s. As I walked to her flat I noticed the two spooks.

Lauren was looking edgy.

"It's good to see you," she said.

"That's nice to know."

"I shouldn't have called you."

"Who are these guys? Can you give me a description?"

"Not really. They're kind of nondescript. But I've noticed them hanging around. When I went out this morning I saw one of them, and when I came back this evening I saw the other one walking after me."

"Nothing else?"

"One of them is kind of burly."

"That's it? They threatened you?"

"No. Nothing like that. Look out the window.

They're there right now." I peered from behind the curtain. "Black Ford. See it?"

"Yeah. I see it."

Typical MI5 monkeys.

"Who are they?"

I shrugged.

"Could be nothing. Don't worry, I'll deal with it for you."

"You're good at dealing with things, aren't you? Who are you Lawrence?"

"A friend, that's all."

"Sure you're nothing more?"

"I could do with a drink."

"I thought you were going to take me out to dinner again."

"You tell me when."

"I start the new job in two days. I've been in to meet them, and they seem really nice. I think I'm going to enjoy working there."

"How about tomorrow night?"

"Dinner? Yes. I've only got vodka."

"Vodka's fine."

She was holding back, but I knew she wanted me to level with her.

"You think they're dangerous?"

"Probably not. But as I say, I'll get rid of them."

She gave me that look again.

"Well, I don't know what I'd do without you right now, Lawrence, even if…"

"What?"

"I don't mean to sound ungrateful, but my life has changed so much in the last couple of weeks since I met you, all in the right direction, you know I wanted out of Global Nexus, especially after what happened, but it's just what with being followed and moving, I feel like someone in one of those government Protection Programmes. My friends are all like 'what'?"

"I know."

"I was going to take a bath, but this got me a little freaked out."

"Why don't you have one now, while I'm here?"

"You don't mind?"

"Go ahead."

While she was out of the room, I called Morris on his private mobile.

I was going to give him the run-around, see what he let slip. Also, I didn't want Lauren knowing she was being watched.

"I need you to move the two guys and replace them by the morning."

"Why?"

"Because they're no good. And make the next two more discreet."

I heard him sigh.

"Very well."

She looked tired after her bath and I suggested she get some sleep.

"I think I will. Thanks for coming round." As I was putting my coat on she said, "The sofa's very comfortable."

"If it makes you feel better. And don't worry, those guys'll be gone tomorrow."

She didn't emerge again until nine thirty. When she did, I'd already seen the black Ford drive off, to be replaced by a grey Lexus now parked at the other end of the road.

I had some breakfast with her and left.

***

I spoke to Morris when I got back.

"I need to know how you're progressing with Spengler."

"I said I'd tell you."

"This isn't moving fast enough."

"Look, this isn't centred on Lauren Smiles."

"Either you fill me in or deal with him."

"We're almost there."

"You don't want this being exposed."

A moment's silence echoed down the line.

"What does that mean?"

"Don't let an innocent party blow it for you."

"Two new men started this morning."

I would give him a few more days and in the meantime continue my own investigation.

Reconnaissance and sabotage helped me out like two old friends.

***

Martoni fed me some more information.

"Klein's a real son of a bitch. Turns out he's been laundering money through British government accounts, and they know."

"That explains a lot."

"He's very good at implicating other people. They can't get rid of him by regular methods because they would all look involved. He's close to Morris. They go way back. And Morris, although not the most senior of secret service personnel, has a lot of strings to his bow. He's good at hustling. Plays down his talents. I'll send you the information through. That's your plot, Jack."

"Thanks, Luca. "

"Well, good luck. Don't get killed, we need you. I'll be in touch."

Martini's information gave me everything I needed.

Morris's career was more interesting than I realised. He'd moved between MI6 and GCHQ. An expert in counter-surveillance, he'd served in the navy and been behind some of the biggest espionage operations since the cold war. He and Klein had been involved in a lot of business together.

Publicly, Klein was just another politician. Privately, he had a cocaine habit and a love of race horses. His wife was a big spender who had never been satisfied with his salary. His lifestyle suggested he was getting something on the side and had been for years: holidays in the South of France, villas in Spain and Italy.

He was nearing retirement and complaining to friends that he'd worked for years with little to show for it. His wife screwed young men, paid for them, and spent his money, telling him she could have done so much better if she'd married someone else. She was some ex-model whose career had died at twenty, who liked a bit of rough and kept him guessing.

Klein regularly hung out the washing, and Morris was his cleaner. They had a cosy outfit going, and the taxpayer paid the commission on any shortfall.

I was sick of the hall of mirrors: them watching me watching them. I started laying traps.

I decided it was time they settled their account.

**

Lauren was enjoying her new job.

When I saw her she looked happy and relaxed.

I asked her how things were.

"Great. Good boss, a woman, which is a welcome relief from roving eyes and hands. Interesting work. Where are we going?"

"A French place near here. That okay?"

"Sure. I'm ravenous. It's good to see you, Lawrence mystery man."

I knew she was curious to find out more about me, and appreciated the fact that she was not pressing me. The few questions she'd asked, I'd dodged.

We had a relaxed dinner and I asked if she'd seen any more suspicious people.

"No. I'd forgotten about it. What did you do?"

"I just warned them off."

"Mm."

I changed the subject.

We talked about her work and her friends.

"They all love the new place and are dying to meet you."

"Oh?"

"You can imagine. New guy takes me out of my old life, puts me in new flat new job."

"When you worked for Spengler-."

"Now, why am I not surprised his name's come up? Yes?"

"Did you ever get to know any of his closest business colleagues?"

"Some. Who are you thinking about?"

"Does the name Klein ring a bell?"

She thought for a moment.

"No. Is he important?"

"Doesn't matter."

It was good that she hadn't had dealings with him.

Back at her flat I could see she was tired. After a drink I left.

"See you soon," she said at the door and gave me a lingering kiss.

"I'll call you."

***

So long as they didn't know I was onto them, I was safe.

One eye on the monkeys, one eye on Lauren, I knew I was going to have to juggle hits while I crawled through the barbed wire.

I was about to carry out a few quick hits rapid as gunfire.

And then the biggest one of all.

No good sitting around drawing attention to myself. I didn't want them guessing.

Just yet.

The Actor

XIX

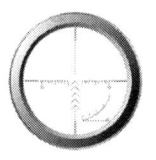

I figured Martoni would make contact and he did.

"I have an assignment for you. Urgent," was all he said when the call came through.

He was staying at Coleridge's and I met him at his suite.

"We need *you* to carry this one out, Jack," he said.

When I opened the file, I almost dropped the photographs.

Staring back at me was an actor I'd seen countless times on screen.

"Are you serious? Marcus O'Neill?"

"I do not joke, my friend." He paused, knowing I needed more information. "There are many things people do not know, many things that go on behind public lines. Before you see the photograph of a much loved, lauded actor, behind the scenes there is a very different story. There is a lot of information in the file. Read through it."

"Fill me in a little more."

"He has offended certain friends who have contacted us for a favour."

"Offended how?"

"The man may be a good actor, for sure. I too have seen him and enjoyed his work, but like many of his kind, old age is something that causes them problems, their masculinity, their sudden lack of desirability among the female population, shall we say, grates on their egos."

"So?"

"This particular man has a big problem."

"Look, many old men find it hard to age, they..."

"What he has done, Jack, is use his status to set up a meeting with a young actress, a girl. Fourteen. He lured her to his hotel room and then forced her to have sex with him."

"He raped a minor, and for that he should go to prison. Why don't the family contact the police?"

"With his Hollywood connections it wouldn't go anywhere, and he knows it. The girl is traumatised, the family have been violated."

"This is high profile."

"He tied her, he burned her."

He waited and watched as I took it in.

I leafed through the file. There was a lot on him.

"She is marked, not just mentally, but physically as well. Scarred. She is not the only one. There are others, all too afraid to speak."

O'Neill specialised in the casual rape and torture of young women. The evidence had been meticulously put together, and from what I could see, this was a fairly open secret in Hollywood.

I put the papers down, my mind on Lauren and Klein's stooges.

"OK then."

"I have your ticket to Hollywood."

I owed him, and so the next day I packed and boarded the first class flight to Los Angeles he had booked me. The brief was to complete by the end of the week, which suited me.

My contact over there was a guy I'd heard Martoni mention on a number of occasions: Lui Simone.

A big mover and shaker among the Los Angeles mob, he met me at the airport and took me to the penthouse apartment I'd be staying in.

It bordered Beverley Hills, and was totally private.

Simone was well-tailored, polite and dead behind the eyes.

"We have this for you, Jack," he said as I set my bags down, handing me some papers and a mobile phone.

"I need transport."

"Downstairs in the parking lot."

"Can you show me where he lives? I know this needs to be done quickly."

"Sure."

My vehicle was a snub-nosed Lexus, and after showing me it Simone drove me to O'Neill's address in his Cadillac. It was a meandering mansion plum in the middle of Beverley Hills. Security gates and guards surrounded the house, ruling out a home hit.

"What else do you need?" he said.

"I'm not sure yet. Time. I want to check out his work-place. Offices, or ..."

"He's filming at the moment."

Can you get me on set?"

"Sure. Anything else?"

"Any idea why the urgency? This is high profile and I need to get it right."

"He's going on a cruise for six months next week, the girl's family want him dead before he leaves."

He left me at the apartment.

The next morning he arrived with a runner's pass to the film set. It was enough to allow me to find out what I needed.

The set was a hive of activity, noisy, neurotic, with everyone focused on the actors: the perfect place for me to hide and go about my business unnoticed.

I carried out the errands I was asked to do without anyone ever questioning me and quickly found O'Neill's trailer.

I didn't sight him until that afternoon when he walked on set: a tall, well-toned old man with a perma-tan glow.

He was late and we were all waiting for him.

The make-up artists danced around him, while the director barked orders at everyone else.

He was fussed over for an hour before we were ready to start filming, and then it was obvious he hadn't learned his lines.

I could see people shaking their heads.

An actor near me walked away in disgust.

"Fucking asshole, he can't even act anymore."

I walked round to his trailer.

There was no one about and it was open.

It was definitely the luxury model, decked out with everything he could want: plasma screens, computers, fridges, Jacuzzi, deep sofas, the lot.

There was nothing in terms of information for me to find out on this assignment, and he kept little of his own affairs lying around.

A box of Viagra stood in the bathroom cabinet, a pair of handcuffs in a drawer in the bedroom.

He obviously had plans for a few sex sessions while filming.

I examined the trailer's potential for the hit: if the blinds were down, as now, it would be secure, but there would be too many people coming and going during the day.

If he was there at night on his own it was a possible, but then he would almost certainly have company.

A hit could be carried out quickly in the bedroom.

There was no other location I could think of, since his house was definitely out of the question.

I left quickly before anyone noticed I was gone.

That evening I called Simone.

"I need to ask a few things."

"I'll tell you what I know."

"Are there any other locations where the hit can be carried out?"

He thought for a few moments.

"It's hard. When he's not on set or at home, he's very much in the public eye. Paparazzi follow him everywhere."

"Anyone he visits?"

"Like a lady?"

"Yes."

"No. He likes them younger. He sometimes does it in hotel rooms, but it's unpredictable, sometimes on set."

"Thanks. I'll be in touch."

It told me what I suspected: it was going to have to happen in his trailer.

***

The next day I checked the security on set. There were a few loopholes.

No one had checked me out, and it wouldn't be hard to come and go unnoticed.

This gave me an opening, but I needed to find out more about O'Neill's habits.

On a day to day basis he pissed the other actors off, butting in on conversations, lording it over lesser talents and messing the director around.

I worked overtime to find out how often he stayed

late in the company of new actresses.

As I helped prepare the set for the next day's shoot I saw a starlet enter his trailer. She looked coked out of her head and couldn't have been more than sixteen.

Half an hour later she emerged followed by O'Neill who languidly entered his chauffeur driven limousine and left.

The next day a young actress came in as her replacement. The starlet had gone into rehab.

When she walked on set it was obvious she was O'Neill's type.

He made a bee-line for her.

He offered to give her a few tips in his trailer.

I sat with a coffee while he chatted to her some metres away.

"I've met many actresses in my time, but you've really got something special."

"Really? Do you really think so, Mr O'Neill?"

"I do."

"Oh, wait till I tell my mom, she has all your films. She's so excited I've got this part."

"Forget your mom, you need to concentrate on your career. I can tell you're gonna be a real big hit."

"Really?"

"And when you do, take my advice, be careful what you say and to who."

"Yes. My mom's always saying that."

"This business is all about reputation and trust, scratch my back, I scratch yours. If you come over to my trailer later, I could take you through your role."

"Would you do that for me? That's fantastic, Mr O'Neill."

"Say about eight," he said, looking at his watch. "It'll be quieter then."

"Oh yes. I'll bring my lines."
"See you there."

He breezed off and barked at someone, reappearing an hour late to fluff more lines.

Time was running out on this hit, and the guy was really making my skin crawl.

***

I knew I had to make this one good and get out before he disappeared on his cruise.

Over lunch I phoned Simone.

"Yes, Jack? How can I help?"

"I need a couple of downers, something strong and dissolvable."

"When?"

"By five. Delivered here."

"I'll get it couriered to you."

***

I worked through the day, keeping an eye on O'Neill and checking for any changes in his arrangement.

At about four I walked into one of the wings and found him with another actress. He had her pinned against the wall. She was struggling as he pressed up against her.

"You're hurting my arm, let go."

"If you snitch, I'll ruin your career."

"Let me go."

"Don't say I haven't warned you."

"You can't treat me like that."

"I can do what I want. There are plenty more like you."

He relaxed his grip and laughed, leaving

fingerprints in her arm.

She stood there rubbing her arm as he walked away.

At five, a bike turned up. I collected the parcel from the rider and went to the toilets to check the contents, enough GBH to get an elephant gang-raped, and fitting. He already had a reputation that was an open secret in Hollywood, the press would make it look like one of his little sessions backfired on him and make a fortune out of peddling the mountain of filth his career sat on.

O'Neill was in the habit of shouting for refreshments at regular intervals throughout the day and at six he said loudly, "Where's the coffee?"

"I'll get that for you Mr O'Neill," I said.

"Bring it to my trailer."

He didn't even look at me and just walked away.

I went back and slipped the two pills into his cup, waited a few minutes and took it through.

I knocked and waited.

He came to the door in a bathrobe.

"Oh," he said, taking it from me and shutting the door.

I went to look for the actress he was planning to see.

It was almost seven when I found her rehearsing her lines.

"Excuse me," I said.

"Yes?"

"Message from Mr O'Neill. He's not feeling well and sends his apologies."

"Oh, he can't make our meeting?"

"No. He says maybe tomorrow."

"Oh well. Tell him I hope he gets better."

"I will."

The set was clearing for the day and by eight there were only a few people around.

When I got to his trailer it was deserted.

I knocked and waited for a few minutes.

No response.

Then, opening the door carefully, I went inside, locking it.

It was dark and he wasn't in the living room.

The door through to the bedroom was closed.

Over on the counter lay the empty cup.

I slowly turned the handle and saw him slouched on the bed in his robe, one leg hanging off the end.

He was out.

I put on my gloves and walked over to him.

He was still breathing when I put my hands around his throat.

Quickly and in one turn I twisted and broke his neck.

He struggled for a brief second just before it snapped, opening his bleary eyes and starting to dribble. His mouth hung open in some mute expression of confused horror as I squeezed.

It took a few minutes while he thrashed about, but I held him hard until all motion ceased.

I then checked for a pulse.

Removing the photos Simone had given me, I left them strewn about his trailer.

Outside, there was no one about.

***

Back at the apartment I called Simone.

"Job's done."

"Good. How did you do you it?"

"Strangulation."

"And the pictures?"

"The press'll have 'em by the morning."

"I'll arrange your flight."

He booked me onto the twelve o'clock back to London.

He drove me to the airport and saw me to the check-in.

As I waited to board, my mobile went.

It was Martoni.

"Another good job, Jack."

"We never discussed terms on this one."

"Say quarter of a million?"

"That's fine."

"I'll wire it through to your account by the end of the week."

On the plane I opened the LA Times.

The leading article read:

"Martin O'Neill found dead in trailer."

Back in London as I unpacked, my phone went.

It was Lauren.

"Hello stranger," she said.

"You okay?"

"Yes."

There was indecision in her voice.

"I've just got back to town. Can I meet you tomorrow?"

We had a candlelit meal with no mention of spooks or Spengler. The interlude I'd engineered was working.

For the moment.

The Goddess

XX

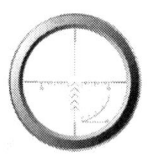

Stella Sharp had been in business a long time before she decided to start her own cult.

Attractive and ruthless, she got sick of only having enough money to go to the South of France twice a year, and only driving a new Mercedes every twelve months.

She'd ditched her husband of ten years and run off with an athlete called Maurice Flame, who she subsequently dumped before working out that she had a gift for making people believe in what she told them.

She had been serially unfaithful to her husband throughout their marriage and he'd never guessed.

When it came to court, she took the lion's share, convincing everyone she was a victim in the marriage, despite the revelations about her infidelities. When her husband tried to make contact several desperate months later, she hired two guys to beat the shit out of him. He later killed himself.

Having studied the New Age, she decided there was good money to be made from it and opened a shop selling New Age Products before beginning a series of lectures, which soon became popular seminars.

By the time I was assigned to her, the Nova Fellowship was several years old, and to all accounts making several million a year.

I'd been called by a wealthy family relative of one

of the cult's devotees.

Thomas Williams was a senior executive with Shell Oil who had worked hard all his life to support an alcoholic wife and two kids. His daughter had married and settled down, while his son Mark, who had a serious drug habit, sponged off him and eventually drifted into the wave spread by the now cruising Nova Fellowship.

I met him in a boardroom at the Shell Offices in London.

He came across as an honest guy who had been stressed for too many years and wore a permanently worried expression. There was pain behind the eyes.

"This is slightly unusual," I said, sitting down.

"I know. Coffee?"

I nodded.

"I received the papers you sent me, but they're not enough to go on. I need contacts and an explanation."

He sat down heavily.

"Where do I start? Two years ago, my son started talking about Stella Sharp. At first I thought she was some girlfriend, then I realised she was running this organisation."

"Cult."

"Yes. He was being dragged into it on a daily basis, and I could see it, but could do nothing. I spoke to various organisations about these groups, and they advised me not to try to persuade him to stay away from them, since that could drive him further into their arms, but to reassure him that I would always be there, and would always accept him. That way if he wanted to leave, it would make it easier."

"Sounds like good advice."

"The problem is, he doesn't."

"Want to leave?"

"Or if he does, he can't."

"Bottom line, you want me to take Sharp out."

He looked down at the carpet.

"She is doing things which ought to put her behind bars. Except, the influence and control she exerts over vulnerable people is extraordinary. I have never met the woman, but I've seen the films. She's got some ability to convince people that I've seen in top salespeople, but there's something else, something she exudes that takes it onto the next level."

"She's running a cult. She's probably very good at it. But at the end of the day your son is exercising his choice to stay there."

I was feeling uneasy about this, wondering if the father wasn't on some ego trip of his own. Also, I'd never taken out a woman before, and it felt like alien territory.

He put his hand up.

"I want you to watch a film. I've already sent someone in there, a detective named Tom Clarke who spent a month undercover and narrowly escaped being beaten up when they discovered he was covertly filming them. Just watch this. Then you can make your mind up."

"All right."

I'd Googled the Nova Fellowship and sat through the usual shit about re-birthing and discovering your inner self, nothing too sinister, nothing out of the ordinary. There were thousands of sites out there saying the same thing in a different language. And there were thousands of suckers wanting to believe it. Whatever rocked your boat.

He put the DVD in the player.

I had no idea what I was about to see.

"This is footage," he said, "Of one of the male groups she conducts. My son is not in this group, but from what I have found out, she separates men and women, controls their sexual habits, and uses this to indoctrinate them with her mind control. If you watch this you will see why I am concerned for my son."

He turned it on.

A group of men stood naked in a room with wall to wall candles. They had cuts and bruises all over their bodies, which were malnourished.

A woman I recognised as Sharp stood at one end with another woman at the other. They both wore robes.

Sharp started giving out orders.

"Kneel," she said.

The men knelt.

"Scum stand."

They stood.

She walked over to each one.

"I own you," she said. "You are nothing. Look at you. Do you desire me? You cannot have me."

The other woman approached from behind.

She handed Sharp a stick. It was a heavy piece of wood with a sharpened end.

"I own your sex," she said. "Don't look at me, you are beneath me."

She started beating them.

The blows were hard, severe. The cuts that were already there opened up, while new ones blistered on their skin. She beat them across the face, crotch, backs of their legs, arms. When she was finished the stick was dripping with blood.

She went over to each of them.

"This is part of your renewal. You have to die in the old way to reach the true woman. Your masculinity has to be broken. Then I can rebuild you. Do you want to be men?" "

Yes," they chanted.

"I will teach you."

"Thank you, Mistress," they said in unison, kneeling while the other woman threw water over them.

The film ended.

"She has torture chambers," Williams said. "Men are kept there, starving, some of them mutilated, for days."

"Do you have evidence of that?"

"No, I have no footage, but Tom Clarke gave me a reliable account."

"Why would anyone join up for this?"

"That's not how it starts. Everyone is lovely at first. That's how Mark described it. There is casual sex on offer from attractive women, drugs are freely available. It's only when you've signed up and gone into one of the temples, that this starts. People don't understand the power these cults have. They use highly sophisticated mind control techniques, many of them derived from the CIA. We seem to be in the middle of a religious crisis, there are so many of them."

"If that's how they treat you once you're in, why stay?"

"By then it's hard to leave. They've bought her philosophy."

"Which is?"

"Man has been a slave master. Man is unhappy because he is carrying the burden of his father's sins. The whole planet's in a mess because of man. She's a goddess and men have to suffer in the same way as women suffered for centuries for things to get better."

He handed me a leaflet.

One line read:

"Women suffered rape, uncaring sex, humiliation, pain, now men enter the cycle and then paradise is found."

"Do you know the whereabouts of your son?"

"He is at what they call Silver Villa."

"Which is where?"

"Hampstead."

"She's going to be hard to reach."

"She's usually there or at the huge house the cult owns in Kensington."

"Why don't you just get him out? Put him through deprogramming."

"Two families tried that recently. Both young men were found by her cronies and killed. Many men disappear in her temples. I want you to take her out and get my son out of there."

I paused. I still wasn't comfortable about taking out a woman, but weighing up what she was guilty of, and measuring it against the freedom of her prisoners, put the job in a different light. There was a reason for this target.

"This will cost," I said.

"I am a wealthy man. I've worked all my life for my family."

"It'll be half a million."

"Fine."

There was not a moment's hesitation.

"And I need all the information you have; contacts, phone numbers."

"It's all here," he said, handing me a list.

"Not just the cult. Anyone from her past?"

"The only person the detective spoke to was a guy called Maurice Flame."

"The athlete?"

"Yes. She had an affair with him before she set the cult up."

"Do you have his details?"

"They're all there."

"I need a retainer."

"How much?"

100k."

"I'll arrange it."

Two days later the money was in my account and I started work.

I was going to hit Sharp as quickly as I could.

XXI

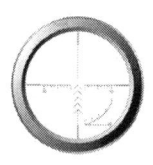

Maurice Flame lived in a rundown flat in Brixton.

Plato road was stacked with drug dealers and students.

I tried his bell several times before he answered.

"Maurice Flame?"

"Who wants to know?"

"I have some money for you."

"I told you, man, stop hassling me."

"Look out of your window."

"Why?"

"I'm not who you think I am."

I waited a few seconds and then saw a head pop out of the first floor.

"So?"

"Remember Tom Clarke?"

"The dick?"

"Yeah. I have something for you."

"What?"

I flashed a wad of cash.

He buzzed me up and I walked up the stairs to his flat.

The living room was full of drugs paraphernalia.

"I told Tom Clarke what he wanted," he said.

He looked out of shape and worn out.

"Still running?"

"You taking the piss?"

"If you can give me some information, I've got a grand here."

"Make it two."

"No."

"What you want to know? About that bitch?"

"Yes." He sat down and lit a cigarette. "You had an affair with her."

"Yeah a long time ago. Wish I never met her."

"Tell me what she was like."

"What she was like? I'll tell you what she was like. A fucking white whore. She liked her meat dark, if you know what I mean. She came onto me, telling me how her husband couldn't get it up. She was all over me at a night club. She took me back to a hotel and fucked my brains out. We used to meet and she'd ask me if I'd kill her husband for her. I was like, what? I used to have something going you know."

"I know."

"So we fuck from time to time, just some white ho wanting it, and when she gets bored she gets nasty."

"Nasty how?"

"I'm not talking about the money, yeah she paid for it, then stopped. She did shit."

"What shit?"

"Drugged me. Cut me, down there."

"Is that it?"

"Isn't that enough? She put cigarettes out on my dick, she fucked me up real bad in the head. She uses people's weaknesses, she preys on people."

"I need everything you've got on her."

"She fucking hates men. She wants to torture them. She's a fucking whore. She should be fucking shot."

"What makes her tick?"

"What makes her fucking tick? I'll tell you what fucking makes that bitch tick - cruelty and power. That's what she eats, see, she loves seeing pain on people's faces, she loves hurting people. Someone should fucking blow her the fuck away."

"What's her weakness?"

"I'm fucked if I know. It ain't sex. She uses it, she fuckin' uses people. If she has one, then it's feeling she's not in control. Yeah, that's it, make her feel she's not in control and she's thrown. Not for long though. I mean, one time I didn't turn up to a date with her, she likes to feel she's got you placed under her finger, and she was shaky. Only until she'd got me in the sack and given me drugs and then..."

"What?"

"Like I said, she likes to hurt people."

"Thank you," I said, and handed him the money.

"Anytime."

XXII

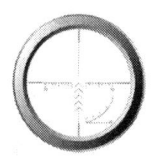

I sat through some of the most tedious talks of my life, my mind on Lauren.

I listened and nodded as mind-controlled robots spoke endless shit about the New Age and spouted spurious philosophy.

Acting this one out was one of the toughest things I'd done. I wanted to get to the target, take her out and collect my money. I had other priorities. I'd cornered Morris, and Klein had gone quiet, but I knew the whole thing was about to blow, and I wanted enough money to get out after I dealt with it.

At first I thought I was over-acting. I just wanted to get there quickly, but these guys were such zombies, I had them fooled from the word go when I rolled up complaining about my rich dad.

I figured they would want a down payment on me, so I handed them 10K apologetically, saying I was due to inherit a couple of mill in a few years time.

They wanted me, and I hooked them in easily.

I'd bought my ticket to the inner sanctum, and when I got there I could see how they worked people.

On my first centre circle session as they called it, a young blonde woman took me through the stages I would have to pass.

The centre circle is what Sharp had christened her

first stage of initiation. There were sixteen of them before men could realise liberation. So far, only a few had reportedly achieved it. I guessed this was propaganda because no one knew who they were. There was going to be a lot of dick-tugging by Sharp and her women before Nirvana was reached.

From what I could see, although the women were not treated well, they were given an easier time than the men. They got to pick and choose who they fucked and sat in on the ritual humiliation of the men, which involved ordering them to perform oral sex on them while they were menstruating, and shitting on them, part of Sharp's philosophy.

That was one of her favourites. She called it the wash.

Her recruiting method was to allow the women to circulate freely, pick up men and form relationships. Lonely guys who would do anything for a shag.

They were instructed to start the humiliation of these guys on the outside so that the passage into the cult was easier. I guess that way Sharp's methods didn't look so odd. She liked to ease the passage.

Sharp's weapon was sex, her mine of gold the soft touch of male desire.

The woman who initiated me into level one started by explaining things to me before standing up and taking off her clothes.

"Do you desire me?" she said.
"Not really."
She looked surprised.
"Why?"
I looked at her.
"I like big busted women."
She left the room.

The next day I was assigned a woman with huge boobs who almost smothered me with them. I said I wasn't interested, figuring this would get me closer to Sharp.

Reject the monkeys and the organ grinder will materialise.

It worked.

Two days later I met her.

XXIII

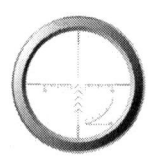

She was pretty much as I'd imagined her to be.

Attractive in a hard, unconventional way.

She dripped with jewellery.

I'd been gathered into a group of what were called the rebels.

These were the guys who didn't go along with what was expected, and who usually ended up being tortured. Unless they had a lot of money, in which case they were treated with kid gloves.

This discrepancy was explained away in terms of their ignorance.

"You are resisting change," she said. "And I want to know why."

We were divided into groups of two and assigned a female analyst who spent a couple of hours asking us questions like "What do you want from a woman?" and "How do you feel about your masculinity?"

I gave vague, meaningless answers and wasted time until the session was over.

I was then left alone in the room with the other guy for a while.

"You got a rich dad too?" I said.

He looked back at me with a dazed expression on his face.

"How did you know?"

"Intuition, I guess."

"That's amazing. People become so in tune here. She's incredible."

I knew what was coming.

The analyst came back after a bit and said, "You need to see Stella tomorrow."

My appointment was for twelve o'clock.

***

I'd slept in a dormitory, eaten beans, salad and endured the biggest pile of shit I'd ever heard in my life. I wanted this job over. I hadn't been able to contact Lauren, since mobile phones and calls were not allowed, and I was worried. I knew she was safe for a while, at least.

I figured the really good-looking guys were kept back for Sharp to fuck and use, and I wasn't wrong.

The only problem was, I hadn't found Williams' son.

The next morning I made use of my free time and headed over to Silver Villa in Hampstead.

I flashed my pass at a fat woman who smelt of BO and walked straight in.

"Come for the seminar?" she said.

"Yes."

"Starts in ten minutes."

"I'll just use the loo."

I explored the house.

I'd heard there was an underground cellar and found it without too much difficulty.

It was a horror story.

Cells annexed the utility rooms and guys were strung up there naked and in a really bad way. The place smelt of shit and misery.

I doubted a couple of them would make it.

One of them was Williams' son.

"Mark?" I said. He opened his eyes and peered at me. "Remember my face. I'm coming back for you later."

"Are you taking me to the next level?"

"Sure am."

I left quickly and made it back to Silver Villa just in time for my seminar.

It had been impossible to sneak any weapons in. I'd managed to acquire an ice-pick on my trip out. It would have to do.

I turned up early for the session with Stella, over at her palatial offices in one of the wings of the place in Kensington.

I could hear groans coming from inside.

I peered in.

She was being serviced by one of the young men she liked, lying naked on a sofa while he screwed her. Occasionally she would give him an order.

After a while she stood up.

"Go," she said and started to get dressed.

She had a used look about her.

I waited outside to be summoned and watched the guy leave, making sure there was no one around.

When I walked in she didn't make eye contact.

I looked around the room. The curtains were drawn.

"Why are you resisting?" she said.

"Oh I don't know, maybe I don't believe it."

She looked up.

"You don't believe?"

"No. It's bullshit. And besides, you're not my type."

Surprise and anger clouded her face.

"How dare you?" she said, standing up. "I will punish you." She picked up one of her sticks and started over for me. "You're going to regret this."

"No. You are."

She swung at me and missed, falling to the floor, the stick landing with a thud.

When she stood up I hit her with the pick. Right in the middle of her forehead. I had it gripped tight and punched it into her head as easily as banging in a nail. I pushed it in deep, her eyes frozen in shock horror as she felt her brains being punctured. Then she fell back with blood pouring from the hole, her mouth moving speechlessly and filling with blood.

I pulled it out, spilling brain matter on the carpet.

She thrashed around for a while in the thickening pool, like she was trying to swim. She tried to speak, but nothing came out. Finally she just collapsed, and lay there.

I went back to my room, got my things and left.

Over at Hampstead I had to knock out a couple of the robots to get back down to the cellars. A couple of easy punches that would leave them nursing headaches when they woke up.

Mark remembered me and I dragged him out of there into the car.

It should have been an easy journey to his father's house, but I hit a road blockade and had to detour. Police cordons were everywhere: apparently a sniper had taken someone out, causing havoc with the local traffic. Once I was out of the detour it was straightforward.

An hour later and he was home.

He scarcely recognised where he was.

"I don't know how to thank you enough," Williams said. "I got your call this morning, so I've prepared everything."

"You need to get a deprogrammer."

"I've already arranged it."

"He needs medical treatment."

"Right. And she's dead?"

"Read the papers tomorrow."

"Thank you," he said. "Your money will be in your account in two days' time."

I said my goodbyes and left.

I really wanted to wash this hit off.

The papers the next morning covered the story with the headline:

"Sex guru killed in horror cult."

It seems the police had found the cellars and shut the Nova Fellowship down.

I called Lauren and arranged to take her out to dinner.

XXIV

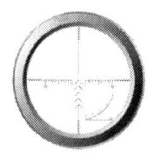

We ate at a restaurant near her flat.

She was pleased to see me and it was good to be in the company of a woman I liked.

She drank a little too much, and I asked her how things had been.

"You know, Lawrence, if that is your real name, we don't really know each other."

"Takes time."

"I'm letting you tell me as much as you want me to know. Or should I say that's safe for me to know." She paused. "I'm not the straightened out woman you see before you today. Or, I haven't always been."

"We all have a past."

"Well, I used to be a real mess. Drugs, casual sex, the whole nine yards."

"You know, this isn't necessary."

"Look, I'm not a fool. I know there's more to you than just some guy who was doing business with Spengler and gets me out of there just before he's killed and the whole mess of what he's involved in is exposed and raked over by the papers."

"If this is about trust, you don't need to..."

"I know. There was a point when I thought I'd just back out of this. But - I like you. We do all have a past. I'm just gonna have to let you tell me or figure it out myself."

"Lauren..."

"I mean even this Lawrence Lauren thing, it's a bit of a tongue twister. Why don't you start by telling me your real name?"

I'd been worrying about her for weeks. I realised how relaxed I felt around her and was sick of patronising her. Sooner or later when the ticking time bomb that was Klein blew, I was going to have to tell her an awful lot.

"Jack," I said.

"Jack. I like it."

"Lauren, there are things..."

"Yeah, there are a lot of things," she said, pouring herself another glass of wine, "And one of them is that I was trying to tell you that ten years ago, I was into everything. I slept with more men than I can remember and now, and now, I just want to find a guy I like and trust. And then you came along and I don't know anything about you."

"It's gonna take time."

"Are you a spy or something?"

"No. I'm not a spy."

"Whatever it is you really do, you're not a businessman. Or not a traditional one."

"When did you clean up your act?"

"Years ago. I only drink now, and I don't sleep with more than one man a week. That's a joke, by the way."

"While I was away, did you notice anyone hanging around?"

"That again? You see, that's the thing about you. I'm just starting to feel comfortable when you start all this cloak and dagger stuff."

I held up a hand.

"Okay."

"So, Jack, how about coming back for a nightcap? I'll tell you if I see any weird guys hanging around."

I walked her back to her flat.

It looked good, a lot of cushions, pictures on the wall. The whole idea of home was alien to me.

She poured a couple of drinks.

"Look, I'm not hassling you, but I can't do all the mystery stuff. I told you a lot about myself tonight, I need you to open up."

"Give it time."

She came over and kissed me on the mouth. She tasted of yearning and desire. The next thing we were fumbling with each other's clothes.

I left the next morning.

XXV

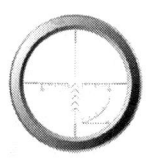

The big names thought they were calling the shots. They wanted to reel me in. And carve me up.

I had other plans. My training in sabotage had been set in stone. I was going to shake the branches. I was going to see how solid they were.

Well, the line broke, the monkeys got choked, and they all went to heaven in a little row boat.

A couple of days later I noticed that the files I held on Spengler had been wiped. I'd known someone had been trying to hack in and finally they'd been successful. My computer was empty.

Except, I'd got a copy of the information. Nothing clumsy, nothing they could know about, no hardware footsteps they could follow. No, I'd snapped the pages onscreen with a digital camera, and downloaded it onto a new laptop.

I'd also set bait: a little time-buying strategy. They'd have seen while browsing my data, that a couple of files had been moved. Files I'd marked Klein and Spengler. Scrambled files. Megabytes of abstract data which meant nothing but which they couldn't penetrate.

While they employed the services of a data miner, I'd start to hunt them. Once they'd figured out all the files held were random figures, I'd be holding a gun to their heads.

So long as they still thought I had something on them I had time. They wouldn't want me dead before they secured all the information they thought I was holding on them.

I'd known it for a few days before I confronted them.

They were sticking to me like glue and I wondered when Klein would put out the word on me.

I was going to send a clear message back to Morris. Destabilize him.

I'd seen the car at the corner of the road, and I'd watched them follow me in and out of supermarkets and on pointless errands.

They were easy enough to set up and they had to be working for Morris.

He still hadn't got back to me concerning Spengler and started dodging my calls.

One morning I went out early, driving just fast enough to make them sweat and then slowing down, so I could corner them.

I drove to a shopping mall, where I wove in and out of shops frustratingly, darted down some escalators and into the gents, dialled a couple of numbers on my mobile in a cafe, ate, let them get hungry, then left.

I drove aimlessly for miles, ending up at a multi-storey car park that I'd never known to be full.

I rapidly accelerated through the floors, stopping abruptly at the top before they could work out what to do.

They were hanging back a few floors below me.

I parked and hid behind some disused boxes. There was no one around.

After about five minutes one guy appeared from the lift, the other on foot.

They looked around, then went over to my car.

One of them was about six four, lean, the other five ten and well-muscled. I couldn't tell if they were tooled up.

"He's not up here," the big one said.

"He must have gone down the stairs pretty fast."

"Do you think he knows we're tailing him?"

"Dunno. Best sit back in the car and follow him out when he returns."

"No, you stay here. I'll just go and check the stairs."

I waited until he was out of sight and then jumped his colleague.

I wasn't going to do any talking, and wanted him out of the way before the other one returned.

He was totally unprepared and I knocked him out clean the first time. I then dragged his body behind the boxes and waited by the doors to the stairs.

When his colleague emerged I grabbed him from behind.

He reached for his weapon but I had him in a lock and heard his arm snap. It sounded like a branch breaking under wet leaves.

I pulled his piece out and flung it.

He was on the ground and I started asking questions.

"Who are you?"

"I don't know what you're talking about."

"One of Morris's boys?"

"You're mad! I was just - Ow!"

I tightened my hold on his bent arm and applied the pressure.

"All right. We were sent to protect you."

"Bollocks, start talking or I'll break the other one."

He was putting up a good struggle and I knew he

wasn't going to sing that easily, so I pulled his other arm up by the shoulder and kicked against the elbow.

The crack reverberated like a gunshot in the empty parking lot.

By now he was screaming. A high-pitched scream more like a little girl's than a man's.

I hauled him over to the edge of the roof and pushed him backwards.

"Talk or you jump."

"We were told to tail you, that's all. We're just following orders."

"From?"

"Morris. We don't know anything else."

"What's your brief?"

"To find out what your movements are. That's all."

"Okay," I said. "You tell your boss to call me in an hour, understand?"

He nodded.

I punched him hard and he fell, then I drove off.

On the floor below I saw their car. I slashed two of their tyres and drove away.

***

An hour later my mobile rang.

Morris was angry, trying to control it.

"You're out of order."

"No. You tail me and avoid my calls, cut me out of the investigation, I'm going to do things my way. What happened to the line of communication? You think you can use me and discard me?"

There was a silence.

"We were trying to protect you."

"Against what?"

"Who. Spengler and his men."

"In case you hadn't noticed, I can take care of myself."

"They're after you."

"Tell me."

"They've ID'd you from Lauren's flat and they're stalking you."

I knew this was a lie and played along.

"I have some information too."

"Then you need to tell us."

I paused.

"Meet me in an hour."

"Where?"

"The Windmill pub, Clapham Common."

He hung up.

I kept him waiting and by the time I arrived he'd had a few whiskies.

I'd never seen him look flustered.

"You know, two of my best men are in hospital."

"Oh dear, cracked a couple of fingernails?"

"One has severe concussion and a broken jaw, the other multiple fracturing of the arm. He won't work for months."

"Tough."

"So what have you got?"

"This is cosy. Don't I get a drink?"

I watched him queue at the bar and got out what I'd put together. A print-out of some of the onscreen shots I'd taken. They'd come out well. It was the tip of the iceberg, but enough to rattle their cages.

I knew it would smoke him out and corner his boss long enough for me to buy myself time.

When he came back I put it on the table.

Everything I had on Klein and Spengler.

His face dropped as he sipped his whiskey.

"This is a conspiracy," he said.

"No."

"Where did you get this from?"

"Let me make this very clear," I said. "Mess with me, and you won't come out of this smelling of roses. I'll blow this thing sky high. When you chose to contact and hire me, you stepped out of your world of espionage and government paid spooks. You're in a criminal world now, we don't play by your rules. I don't care much for the government and its pack of liars, or for your ways. There's more honour among gangsters than your crowd. I am not disposable, and you better start realizing that."

"Do you know what powers we have?"

"Sure. But then again, if you don't come out of this looking clean and drawing your pension, you may not come out of it at all. Kill me, and I'll send someone after you. I've already put that contingency plan in motion. Anything strange happens to me, and you're the next hit. That goes for Lauren too, she better be protected properly by your guys."

I watched a small vein throb at the corner of his temple. He raised his glass with the measured slowness of someone trying to control his shaking hands. Klein was breathing down his neck, I could smell him.

"I've put our best men on the job."

"Yeah well they beat the first couple of monkeys, but make sure she's safe, that's all."

He was not used to being given orders.

"Now, going back to Klein," I said. "This is the deal. You leave me alone and ensure Lauren's safety until Spengler's dealt with and anyone who may be connected to this thing, and it's over. I'll bury this. One false step, and it'll go straight to the media."

"That's it?"

"No. I've got more on him and you and you don't know where to find it. Let's call it a little insurance policy I'm holding in case you start playing games.

"We could come to some sort of financial arrangement."

"No. You've paid me for what I've done, but I'm not doing any more for you. Those are my terms. Do we have an agreement?"

"Okay."

"And the other thing."

"Yes?"

"Keep me informed about the progress on Spengler. I want to know everything."

"All right."

"Why is it taking so long?"

"It's complicated."

"By the fact that Klein doesn't want to be exposed."

He said nothing and I walked away.

***

I kept a regular eye on Lauren, taking her out to dinner and making sure the spooks were still watching her.

She didn't mention anyone following her. I wondered when she would notice.

***

A few days after our meeting Morris called me.

"I have news," he said.

"Good."

"We're taking Spengler out tomorrow."
"How?"
"Explosion."
"What about his cronies?"
"Them too. There is a meeting taking place, and we have very good information they will all be there. They won't survive."

***

I saw it on the news. A fire bomb of a story.

The entire wing of a restaurant was blown apart. Spengler and Hinch had taken a private table away from the other diners. They'd made it look like a terrorist attack. Two waiters and a couple of members of the public went down with them. Killing two birds with one stone, I guess.

Sloppy, but they'd taken care of them. And the innocent blood was on government hands.

The headlines in the papers the next day read:

"Police too slow to act on Al Jaeda threat. No warning for diners as lethal bomb blast tears through restaurant."

The pictures showed the web of tangled metal and shattered glass. The deep stains on the restaurant floor.

Reporters mobbed the area and the official story stuck in the public mind. The lie stuck like a fishbone in my throat.

"The matter is over," Morris said when he called.

"Seems like it. Messy job, though. But then, what do you care about a few civilians when you get some free propaganda in?"

"We're taking the men off Lauren and this closes the case."

"It better. If there's anyone you've missed and

they come for me, I'll come after you."

He hung up.

I'd bought myself time, but not much.

***

Later that day Lauren called me.

Her voice was shaky, far away.

"Did you see the news?"

"The bomb?"

"Yes. Spengler was one of the diners."

"Yeah, I've just heard."

"That's spooky."

"He was mixing with the wrong crowd. That's why I was so keen to get you out of there."

There was a pause full of thoughts that echoed. I knew where this conversation was going.

"Who are you?"

"A friend."

"With some powerful connections, it would seem. I don't like being kept in the dark, Jack."

"Trust me," I said.

"Why?"

"I've helped you, haven't I?"

"Yes. But I'm not stupid."

"It would be good to see you."

"Give me some time."

***

I checked the facts and it seemed Morris was telling the truth.

Spengler and his key men were dead.

If anyone tailed me now, they had to be sent by

Klein.

XXVI

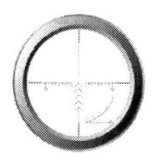

I spent a lazy weekend at Lauren's flat.

It was disconcerting, feeling at home after all the years of hits and hotel rooms.

She'd backed off a little and didn't ask any questions about my past. There was a lull. The line was lying still on the surface of the water, and I knew something was about to break soon. I wanted to be ready.

Work was quiet, so I took her away for a week to the Caymen Islands.

I needed to bank all that cash.

We sunned ourselves, swam and got on as if we'd known each other for years. If she had her suspicions, she kept them to herself. For the time being.

The night before we were due to return she said:

"You know, glad as I am that I met you, Jack, we've got to stop this *charade*." I looked at her. "I think I know what you do, and it's just a matter of time before you open up to me."

I wasn't sure if she did, but I let the matter lie.

I dropped her back at her flat when we landed and she returned to her work.

I'd been doing a lot of thinking about my life and where it was heading. At the end of that week she called me.

"There are some guys hanging around."

I'd been expecting it a long time.

Unable to find me, they were using her as a tracking device.

I drove round and knew immediately they weren't spooks.

I called her from my mobile.

"Don't worry, I'm taking care of it. How long have they been there?"

"I don't know. I thought I was imagining it at first, you know, being paranoid, then I realised they were definitely tailing me."

"They follow you to work?"

"I lost them. That's why they're outside. Who are they?"

"I'll tell you when I know. In the meantime, relax, if you look out of the window you'll see my car."

"Oh." I saw a curtain twitch. "Okay."

"I'll be here for a while. Only call me mobile-to-mobile."

I watched them for hours.

One guy, the bigger one, got out for a pee. He disappeared behind some houses and returned lighting a cigarette. He wore his collar up and had a thick growth of beard.

The other one went for some coffee. He had a tattoo on his hand.

Finally, they drove away at midnight.

I followed from a distance.

After an hour the car pulled up at a house in White City. The guy with the tattoo got out.

I followed the car for a further twenty minutes or so as it wove its way into Hammersmith. Finally it stopped in the street outside some flats.

I parked on the other side of the road as the big

guy got out and started walking. I followed and jumped him as he was fumbling for his keys by the stairs to a darkened basement.

He went crashing down headfirst and landed badly.

I jumped on him and kicked him hard enough to break a few bones.

"What do you want with Lauren Smiles?"

"Okay! Okay! Fuck! You've broken my arm."

"That's not all I'll break if you don't start giving me some answers."

"I'm just following orders."

"Whose orders?"

"I don't know."

I hit him so hard he started to cough blood.

"Whose orders?"

"Klein."

"Well tell him to back off. And tell your buddy if he doesn't back off, I'll do him too, understand?"

"I understand."

"If I hear you've been hassling her again, I'll kill you, and it won't be pleasant. Right?"

"Right."

I hit him again for good measure and left him staggering around in his own blood before going back to Lauren.

I reassured her everything was okay, and they were gone.

"Just tell me immediately next time if you see anything," I said.

"I hope there isn't one. Thank you, Jack, although, I don't know who to fear more, you or them. I saw those guys."

"I think you know the answer to that."

I left her, knowing it was time to reel Klein in.

The Entrepreneur

XXVII

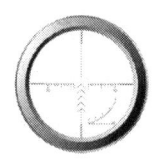

I called on Martoni for a few favours, and he came back to me with a major hit.

I needed information which only he could give me. Personal details about Klein.

I was going to start with Morris. He and Klein were like Siamese twins looking for money in a sewer.

I wanted these two guys hurt and out of my life and Lauren's. I was going to grab that line and pull them down. Down into my world, into its waters.

I'd begun to see a future for myself beyond the hits.

Martoni, as usual, got everything I needed: addresses, personal bank details, past connections and present ones.

"I hope it helps, Jack," he said. "And I have something for you."

I'd seen this coming. I arranged to meet him the next day.

I was going to be busy.

***

He was staying at the Lanesborough.

"This is an unusual one Jack, and at first I was a little put off by it."

He passed me the file.

Inside it were pictures of a woman. Hard as reinforced steel. About as feminine as a suit of armour. As I leafed through the dossier, he gave me the brief.

"Trudi Stein, a very wealthy woman. Started in retail, to all intents and purposes, and moved her way up through a property empire. She now has her finger in various pies."

"Business rivalry?"

"No. I am all for people doing well. This is for a client."

"So, what then?"

"She is not all she seems and the reason there is a contract out on her is because of something else."

I looked though the documents he'd enclosed and began to see Stein was involved in a lot she wouldn't want her name connected to: sweat shops, people trafficking and a lot more.

"She has many companies. How she started was as a Madame. Her girls hated her, and remember her to this day with loathing. She had them beaten up, paid them hardly anything and set them up with very violent customers. They felt she had some sadistic kick, enjoyed seeing them hurt."

"And now?"

"That's behind her, but you see some of it in the file there. She rips off anyone who gets in her way. And if she can't rip them off, she has them removed. Millions have been stolen by her over the years. Also, she has muscled in on the drug market."

"Competition?"

He shook his head again.

"More than that."

"What is it she has done to your client?"

"She owes him money, firstly. That in itself would not have been enough for me to contact you."

"How much?"

"Two million dollars."

"But this is more than debt collection."

"She was employing his daughter at one of her companies. A very intelligent, attractive woman with a big future in front of her. She was a lawyer and stumbled across something on Stein. She wouldn't let it drop. She expected to be sacked, but no, she was sent on a business trip, all expenses paid to Columbia."

"Straight into a trap."

"She didn't just have her killed. She enjoys seeing people suffer. She wanted it to look like a random attack. She was raped repeatedly and tortured, left to die in a hole in the ground. She was pregnant. My client is willing to pay two million."

The idea of carrying out a hit on a female target was still uncomfortable to me. But then, was Stein any better than Sharp? I thought for a minute, knowing Martoni expected reciprocity for what he'd done for me, and considering there was nothing in the job to stop me doing it. What I was weighing up was how much time it would leave me to deal with other matters.

"I need an expense account."

"We can set one up for, say, 150K."

"That'll do for the moment."

***

Reading up on Stein was instructive: she was a seriously ruthless businesswoman with no friends and a lot more money than she was letting on.

The pictures of her various victims said it all. She

was a vicious bitch.

A lot of people had disappeared over the years. Business contacts who got in her way were sent to out of the way places where criminal investigation was not well developed and the murder of foreigners not considered a priority.

Her offices stretched from London to New York, via just about every major European city.

She could usually be found at the offices of MultiTec when in London, a huge building in the Docklands.

I decided to pay it a visit.

**

The security was tight and I couldn't get past reception.

A hard-nosed woman in her early thirties asked me who I was there to see and when the name I gave bounced, said, "He says he's never heard of you. What is the nature of your business?"

"I have some business to put MultiTec's way."

"Who do you work for?"

"Look, there has to be some misunderstanding. I was given an appointment at this time. Now, can I see someone, please?"

She got on the phone.

"He won't say who he works for…Yes, I know. All right."

She hung up.

"If you could leave your personal details, then someone will call you back."

"I've come all this way on good faith."

"Unfortunately, we do not have any record of your appointment."

"That's not very impressive."

She looked irritated and handed me a pad and pen.

"If you could put your details down here, someone will be in touch."

I gave her a mobile number and left.

A man called Tom Drake rang me later that day.

"I believe there was some mix up over an appointment. We've checked our details, but really can't see any record of it."

"I have some contacts in South America who are interested in liaising with Mrs. Stein."

"Which part of South America?"

"Venezuela, Bolivia mainly."

"And what is the nature of the business?"

"Forestry and development."

Stein was buying a lot of land in South America and I hoped this would drop enough of a hint or bait when he reported it back to her.

"That's interesting. I'm not sure if we would get involved in that, but I'll find out and get back to you."

He did.

The next morning, my phone went bright and early.

He asked me if I could come in again, and we arranged an appointment for the next day. Martoni helped me with a list of credible contacts and I spent the best part of the day putting together a business proposition.

I spent the evening with Lauren, who appeared relaxed and happy.

No mention of any stooges, but I knew replacements were on their way.

***

Tom Drake went through a polite routine with me that basically amounted to fobbing me off while pretending to listen to my pitch. He'd obviously not mentioned me to Stein.

"That's very interesting," he said after half an hour, getting to his feet dismissively.

"I have one more thing I want to show you", I said, and passed him some contacts in Bolivia.

He paused and looked intently at me.

"Could you leave these with me?"

"No."

"Hold on a minute."

He put the file down and left the room.

A few minutes later he returned.

"I have a list of free times for Mrs. Stein, perhaps we can arrange an appointment for you to see her?"

"Sure."

He booked me in for the end of the week and looking at me with angry respect saw me out of the building.

Driving back I saw an army of flashing lights. The sniper had struck again and the police were tightening security.

XXVIII

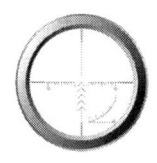

I checked out her house.

    A huge place in 'The Boltons'.

    Surveillance paid off: I could see a few ways in.

    So far the offices at MultiTec looked a no-go for carrying out the hit.

    I saw Lauren and made sure she wasn't being followed and waited for my appointment. In the meantime, I did more digging around Klein.

    He was doing a lot of business with Russia. I guessed it wasn't the government that was funding his purchase of a Lear Jet.

    A couple of the names he was mixing with were definitely Russian Mafia. A greedy guy like that had a habit of pissing people off. His government connections weren't going to count for anything in that world. The more dirt surrounding him, the better my camouflage.

    Morris carried out whatever he asked him to do.

    A few days later and the stooges were back. Two new guys who were slightly less conspicuous than the first pair.

    Lauren didn't notice them, but I did.

    I said nothing to her, and instead tracked them home one night and beat the shit out of them. One at a time, leaving them needing hospital treatment.

    The message was certainly getting back to Klein.

The next day I met Stein over at MultiTec.

She was an ugly, superficially charming woman who had a razor-sharp business brain and a voice like breaking glass.

Dressed from head to toe in designer gear she ushered me into her office. It was as big as an apartment and commendations and awards lined the walls.

"I believe you have some contacts in Bolivia," she said by way of opening.

"I showed them to your colleague."

"Could I have a look?"

I passed her the file, and she pored over it for a while.

"This could be very useful to us. How much do you know of what we are planning in South America?"

I knew she would be trying to find out why I'd approached her with this and noticed how intently she was looking at me.

"Not much. I know you've been trading with Colombia."

"Oh?"

"The natural resources in South America must be extremely useful to a company like MultiTec."

"They are."

"So are you interested? I do have other parties."

"What are you proposing?"

"We set up a joint trading venture. I hand my contacts over to you for a part of the trade."

"How much?"

"Say, ten percent."

I knew she would jump at that.

"That sounds okay. And your involvement?"

"Minimal. As much as you want."

"Then I think we can draw up some initial plans",

she said.

We shook hands and arranged another appointment.

I'd seen most of the building, but used the opportunity to ask a few questions.

"I can ask one of my staff to show you around, if you're interested," she said.

Exactly what I wanted. Except, the tour ruled the offices out once and for all, the security was like Fort Knox. The hit would be at her house.

I knew she would have me checked out.

But I was moving too quickly for her. This was my fastest hit.

One evening after spending time with Lauren I paid another visit to The Boltons.

It was gone two when I got there and parking round the corner I decided on a trial run. The garden looked the best option.

I disabled the sensor lights and climbed over the gate.

I had a quick look round and saw that one of the windows was forcible, then I hightailed it out of there before anyone stirred.

***

Then Lauren called me one morning.

I could hear fear in her voice.

"Jack, they're back."

"The same guys?"

"No different ones. They've been out there all night."

"Get a taxi to work and I'll meet you there later. What time do you finish?"

"About six."

"Don't leave until I've turned up."

I drove round and saw them.

This time I was going to try something different.

As they went off for some lunch, I called a contact of mine for a favour. He turned up within minutes.

I levered their door open and removed their parking permit.

Then he towed their car away, putting it in the pound.

When I met Lauren I suggested she spend the night at my Mayfair penthouse.

I went out for some groceries and she made dinner. I was trying to keep her calm, which was getting harder.

The next morning I took her in to work and drove by her place to check if the stooges were back.

No sign of them.

***

Around this time the papers were filled with news of the sniper. It looked like we had a new serial killer on the loose: there had been several deaths in major cities across the country in addition to the two in London and reading the profile, the guy struck me from the off as a pro.

XXIX

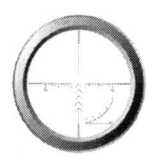

Stein was getting suspicious.

I had twenty-four hours until our appointment and avoiding it seemed the best option. There was only one way to do that.

Martoni phoned, saying that she was planning something big in Colombia and the interests of another client were threatened. He wanted her stopped and fast. So did I.

I looked at her file again and thought about the young woman she'd got raped and tortured.

I analysed the information on Stein, her habits. The Google earth shots I had showed she had a habit of watering her roof garden at night. Her husband was away on business and her kids were all grown up. Staff came and went at her house, but Saturday nights she'd spend alone if she wasn't entertaining.

There was no reason to delay.

I turned up at eleven, parked round the corner then disabled the sensor lights and climbed into the back garden.

I could see she had guests.

A cosmopolitan crowd was assembled there; many of them looked South American.

I waited until gone midnight and watched them leave one by one.

It needed to look like an accident.

After a while, true to habit, she went up onto her roof terrace.

As the lights went on up there I jemmied the window at the side and climbed in.

I changed shoes.

It was two flights up and when I got there the door was open. She had her back to me.

She'd been drinking all night and was wobbling slightly as she hosed her plants down.

I waited until she went right over to the edge, and sneaking up behind her, pushed her in the back.

She staggered and went over the first time. I didn't need to exert much force, so there would be no pre-impact bruising.

I saw her crash below onto the patio.

I went back down and left the way I came.

She lay there in a pool of blood with the watering can next to her.

I left and walked back to the car round the corner.

I changed my shoes and drove away.

***

The next day I called Martoni.

"It's done."

"A fall, I hear. Nice touch."

A few days later the money came through to my account. By then, I was busy with Klein.

Klein

XXX

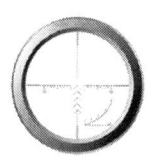

The ace I held were the pictures I took of those files from Global Nexus. Klein was angry now he knew the scrambled files were a hoax, but he was going to stop me leaking what I still had to the press.

I still had my uses alive.
The stooges came back.
This time in another car.
I cut their break wires.
They didn't die, but Klein's hands started to shake.
He'd also found out my address.
I saw the car outside and turned round.
I booked into a hotel.
Late that night I ambushed them.
They were livelier than the previous ones.

I caught them trying to break into my apartment when I hit one of them with a cosh. He went down cold and I fought the other guy for a while.

Eventually I knocked him out with a broken jaw.
I needed to get to Klein fast.
The next day I went over to his address.

The security was so tight it would be impossible to get in. And I knew approaching him at his place of work would be out of the question.

So I laid another trap. My biggest weapon against Klein was information.

Everything Martoni had given me added up to a nice little bit of time in prison for him and Morris. I had recordings of his deals and financial details. If the papers bit, then the police would have to investigate.

I took a package round to the offices of The Sun and handed it in anonymously.

I requested no fee and the editor happily took it off me.

I wanted to destabilize them.

I spent a couple of days at Lauren's flat and watched the next car drive up.

***

I'd been thinking of retiring and leaving England, so when Martoni called and told me about some property in Sicily I couldn't resist.

I looked at the portfolio he sent over and immediately spotted the perfect place: a large villa near enough to a town, but quiet. It was reasonably priced and I knew the area. I thought it would prove a useful bolt-hole for Lauren and me when Klein and Morris were exposed by the British press.

Lauren was getting edgy again and I suspected she'd noticed the car which was parked in her street every day.

She said she was being followed to work again and I began to wonder if The Sun was going to bite.

Then, one morning I bought the papers. Two headlines dominated them.

The first read:

Government minister in arms deal scandal

A major cabinet member has been conducting covert and illegal arms negotiations with rogue states.

I felt a sense of relief.

The second leading story was about the serial killer.

The headline read:

"Killer strikes again: two ministers shot dead on their doorstep."

XXXI

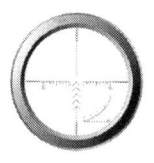

The story flooded the tabloids.

The government immediately suspended Klein and conducted an investigation into the dealings. Junior ministers resigned and there were calls for a police enquiry.

And it followed.

Morris was the first to be dragged across the coals. He wasn't saying anything, refusing to give away his boss, but the pressure was obviously getting to him.

I had him figured as another guy waiting for his pension. I didn't fancy his chances. The paparazzi smelt blood and were circling him like a wounded animal.

Meanwhile, Lauren began to piece things together. She didn't say anything directly to me, knowing I was watching her back.

I told her I'd bought a place in Sicily and asked her if she fancied a holiday.

We were living together during this time.

Meanwhile, the serial killer continued to strike.

The body count was rising rapidly and the more I read about him, the more I saw the signature of a trained gunman.

There was more to the story and I knew it, except I only had one eye on it.

***

A few weeks later Klein was questioned by the police.

His picture was plastered all over the Sunday papers, and by the look on his face he wasn't enjoying the attention.

The material added up and the stories made it clear he was guilty.

His ministerial post was gone and taken by someone else. He had the look of a man who knew it was over and was looking at time.

He was the kind of guy who operated by using and setting up others, so Morris was the obvious fall guy. He"d been routinely questioned, but his tight-lipped response meant that a lot was going to be decided in court. And that was exactly where it was heading.

Then, two things happened in the space of twenty-four hours which would change the course of events irrevocably.

The killer struck again with another sniper shot. The victim Morris.

As he was picking the milk from his doorstep, the shooter picked him off, leaving his brains all over the porch.

I caught the story in the evening paper on my way back to meet Lauren at her office.

When I got there reception informed me she had gone out for lunch and hadn't returned.

***

At midnight there was still no sign of her at my apartment and I knew they had her.

By then I'd pieced it all together.

Morris's death was to order: the serial killer was a

hired assassin working for Klein.

I sat down and Googled the news coverage from when the story broke.

For months now, key industrial and political figures had been dying. A few red herrings had been thrown into the stew just to confuse people: a wino here, a shopper there. Some of the others were interesting: a leading director who was just about to start shooting a film about arms dealing. Another victim was a government auditor who had a reputation for whistleblowing.

Morris had taken the bullet for Klein and I wasn't about to let Lauren be the next victim. Someone would make contact. What Klein wanted more than anything else was his reputation and freedom back. With Lauren alive he had some bargaining power with me.

XXXII

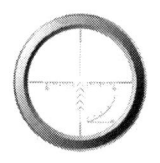

When the call came it was from Lauren.

She was struggling to sound calm, but the fear was there.

"Jack, it's okay. I'm not hurt."

"You sure?"

"Yes. They want you to meet them, to hand over what it is you're holding on them. If you do that, they'll let me go."

"Where and when?"

"They'll call you. They said to tell you to get everything you've got and bring it with you when you meet with them."

"Okay."

"And they say just you on your own."

"Okay."

"Jack, you're the only person I can trust in this..."

The line went dead. They were going to let me dangle. I'd use the time.

I knew what they wanted: the missing snapshots. They had everything else. My apartment had been ransacked and all computers and files removed. But I had the memory card.

I also knew if I gave them what they wanted, they'd kill Lauren.

I'd never felt angrier than when I put that phone

down. All the hits I'd carried out I'd done with professional detachment, scumbags who deserved to be wasted.

Now I had a personal motive.

I needed to know who was holding Lauren.

Fast.

I'd never wanted to carry out a hit so much, and this time I wasn't going to get paid.

They were going down, and I was going to put them in a death spiral.

***

I spent twenty-four hours staking out Klein's house.

The gates only opened twice, once to admit a limousine with blacked-out windows, once a van.

I saw no sign of him.

The gates shut out the outside world and I couldn't make out if he was even there.

I knew he had staff and kept irregular hours, but beyond this little else. He was a secretive man.

He had to be in contact with his hired help and the only way to find Lauren was to follow him or bug his calls.

He wasn't going to let himself be tracked. The paparazzi were pursuing him and he wasn't going to hand them any juicy shots.

The kidnapper was keeping him updated by phone.

I bugged his lines, but the only thing I heard was his wife calling friends, complaining about the press intrusion into their lives, and Klein talking shop with a few business colleagues.

He wasn't giving anything away.

I'd guessed he would probably make his important

calls on a mobile and I was right.

Then, bright and early the next morning, the second call came through.

A man's voice said, "One o'clock, bring everything we need."

"I give you this, I want Lauren there. And she leaves with me."

"You're not calling the shots."

"That's the deal. I have more information which hasn't reached the papers yet."

He didn't know if I was bluffing.

"You'll see her when you hand it over."

"No. I arrive and show you what I've got. Then you give me Lauren. I don't hand anything over until then."

There was a pause.

Then the line went dead.

This would smoke Klein out. A man as secretive as him wouldn't discuss anything important over the phone, even a mobile.

He would be at his office, so I drove straight round there and waited.

Just as my mobile went, his car drove out of the parking lot.

I followed.

"Hello?"

"Okay. But you bring everything."

The meeting was two hours away and I was gambling that my ruse had forced a meeting between Klein and his accomplice.

His car meandered in and out of traffic, going downtown towards Kennington. Then it turned into Battersea. It stopped outside some flats.

Klein got out and went down some steps into a basement.

He came out a few minutes later with a guy in a track suit.

He was heavily built and had the upright gait of someone ex-military.

I followed them to some lock-ups on the edge of an industrial wasteland, hiding my car.

There was a row of units looking over onto some gasworks.

They walked round the corner and walked back.

I parked on the corner and watched as the guy in the track suit opened one of them and they went inside.

Half an hour later they emerged.

Klein was saying something and it got pretty heated.

His accomplice got on his mobile.

Mine rang.

I had them.

I waited.

Just before it went to voicemail I answered.

"Yes?"

"The time's been changed."

"When?"

"Two."

"Where?"

He gave me an address which I recognised as the basement flat I'd seen Klein pick him up from.

I watched them drive off and then went over to the lock-up.

There was no sign outside.

I looked around. The place was deserted.

I walked back to my car and returned with a jemmy.

The door wrenched open pretty easily and I went inside.

I found the light and walked past piles of boxes to the office at the back.

The glass door had a blind pulled on the other side.

It was locked.

There was nowhere else to hide someone.

I kicked it in and found Lauren tied and gagged in the corner.

She looked terrified but when she saw it was me her expression mellowed to relief.

I freed her legs and arms and pulled the industrial tape off.

"Thank God," she said and threw her arms around me.

"Are you okay?"

"Yes. I mean, shaken up but he didn't hurt me."

"Come on, let's get you out of here."

She was shaking and I got her into my car and drove her to my flat.

I fed her and made sure she wasn't hurt.

She was telling the truth.

I'd got to her just in time.

XXXIII

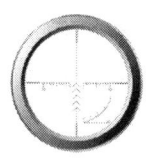

I checked us into a hotel, and after eating, she had a bath.

By now the deadline had passed, but it no longer mattered.

When my phone went, the voice sounded angry.

"Do you want us to hurt her? Why didn't you show?"

"I got held up. I can make it later."

He hung up.

Lauren came out of the bathroom in a robe, drying her hair.

"Do you know what I really want right now, Jack?"

"You name it."

"A drink."

I poured her a brandy.

"You know, when I've recovered, I've got a few questions to ask you, and you're gonna answer them."

I just watched her until she started to fall asleep.

Then I went out.

By now it was late.

They would have found that she'd gone.

I made my way over to the basement flat.

When I got there I could see a light.

I waited until he came out.

He was carrying a case. Just the right size for a

gun.

I followed him to another address a few miles away. He went in for the night and after a few hours I guessed he wouldn't emerge again until morning.

Klein's orders must have been to relocate then kill me and Lauren.

I figured he would go to my penthouse first, so I headed straight to her flat. The place was exactly as she'd left it.

I'd read through everything on the net about the serial killer and re-examined his profile.

The papers were giving out this picture of the sordid world of an embittered professional, coming up with theories of a failed politician with a grudge.

Klein's intention had obviously been to throw as many red herrings out there as people would swallow. And people had eaten this one whole and were queuing up for more.

Psychologists were spouting the same old stuff about personality disorders and abused childhoods, the same old yarn. I knew differently. The whole media machine was being used to distort the truth and protect the people at the top.

The only thing they were getting right was that this guy was a pro, and I knew his background was military.

Klein had thought this through carefully and hand-picked him.

He could remove any obstacles to his success as an arms dealer by setting up the smokescreen of a serial killer on the rampage, and take out his enemies.

I knew that if Klein was pushed, the killer would be told to act quickly.

So the first thing I did was call him.

At nine o'clock I rang straight through to his

offices and he picked up.

"Klein?"

"Yes."

"I'm going to drop a much bigger bombshell today, one that will see you put away for good."

"Who is this?"

"You know who I am."

"Are you threatening me?"

He was wary of being bugged and wasn't going to say much, but it didn't matter.

"I'm at Lauren's flat."

"Who's Lauren?"

I hung up, knowing he would get straight on the phone to his accomplice.

I left a note which read:

"Location: Oxford Street, McDonalds. Time: 12.00."

Nice and busy.

It would provide cover and publicity.

In the boot of my car I had an Armalite AR-10, the weapon favoured by the serial killer who by now would be racing towards Lauren's flat.

XXXIV

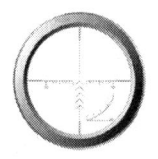

Martoni had some offices just opposite the McDonalds.

I knew they were empty and I'd already cleared it with him: I could use them and had the keys.

I went straight there and up to the top floor of the building.

The entire floor below was unoccupied.

I locked the door and made my way over to the window.

I had the McDonalds in my sights.

Then I waited.

There was a thick crowd below. People milling around, dropping litter, eating burgers, dodging one another, busy with their shopping, talking on their mobiles.

The killer had often picked people off in a throng, and this hit was going to bear all the hallmarks of one of his shootings.

He took his time.

What neither he nor Klein were aware of was that I knew what he looked like.

And after an hour I saw him.

He was wearing a pin-striped suit and looked quite different, but it was him all right.

You can tell if someone's carrying a weapon. There is a definite gun gait you can spot. He was tooled up with a handgun.

He walked up to the McDonalds and then stopped.

Then he went inside.

I focused the rifle on the door.

I squared the telescopic lens on it and waited.

A few minutes later he came out and started walking away. I put the cross hair on his forehead, he was walking towards me. That made it easier.

I waited till he passed a group of tourists, then fired.

All it took was one shot. The rifle gave a gentle hiccup. He went down like a tree and just lay there while the crowds stepped over him until someone noticed the pool of blood spilling across the pavement. Then a woman stopped and held her hands to her face.

She had brain matter on her dress. Another woman noticed the thick stains on her blouse and started screaming. The short, sharp, staccato noises broke the air and sounded like a siren.

A group formed while others stood back and watched.

People got on their mobiles.

I put my rifle in the hold-all and went out into the deserted hallway.

Then I left by the rear exit and walked to my car.

I was out of there before the police arrived.

XXXV

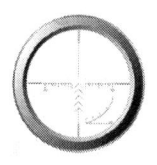

At the hotel Lauren was okay, if a little drunk.

"It's over," I said.

"Really?"

"Really."

We had some lunch at the hotel. I'd started to think about how I could tell her who I was and realised it was not going to be in this country.

***

Later that night I called Klein.

All I said was, "The package is now in the hands of the press and the police." I then hung up.

I'd left the memory card at the offices of *The Sun*.

They had one very happy editor.

If the police didn't get to him quickly, then I'd take him out. Without his sniper, he was for the moment just another wounded politician avoiding further publicity.

The following morning I went over to Lauren's place on my own.

No one tailed me.

I wanted to clear it up before she saw any mess.

It wasn't too bad.

The front door had been kicked in and a few drawers emptied onto the floor, but that was about it. I hadn't given him enough time to cause too much damage.

I called a carpenter and a locksmith and tidied the rest up myself.

***

The papers really got their teeth into this one.

One front page read:

Mad killer shoots businessman from rooftop in Oxford Street.

The theories multiplied and no one had the slightest clue what had really happened.

No one ever got to know who the latest victim was. His identity had been surgically removed by virtue of his job.

What the police didn't know was that there would be no more murders from the guy they were looking for.

He'd been killed with his own signature.

And the papers were about to get a whole lot busier with the breaking news about Klein.

XXXVI

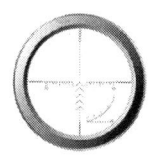

He saved me the trouble.

A few days later I read in the papers that Klein had killed himself, a bottle of booze and pills by his bed.

The headline read:

"Disgraced government minister's body found by wife."

Guys like that, operating from a safe distance of spin and professional exploitation find exposure hard to bear.

He never got to read the scoop.

The story lasted for weeks, and they picked over his bones until they were bleached white.

He'd certainly made a name for himself.

***

Lauren started to recover from her ordeal. We moved out of the hotel and into my apartment.

Martoni called me one morning and told me the villa was all mine.

"You can pick up the keys any time," he said. "It would be good to see you."

This seemed the perfect opportunity to retire.

I ran the idea of a holiday past Lauren.

"I could do with a break," she said.

"How about work?"

"I could do with a break from that too."

"We could go out there and spend some time, see if you like it, maybe live there a while."

"That sounds great. And we can talk."

"Sure. I'll book the tickets."

I realised I'd run out of manoeuvring space and didn't care.

The next day I put my place on the market.

**

On the plane, I looked over at Lauren and said, "I think I might take some time off work too."

"Whatever that is."

"I hope you like Sicily."

"I hope so too. Do you know anyone out there?"

"I do have a contact."

"Now why doesn't that surprise me?" she said.

Below, the earth looked green and good.

Outside only azure sky.

We landed and stepped out into the wall of heat.

A message from Martoni was waiting for me on my mobile.

21496433R00134

Printed in Great Britain
by Amazon